These Wrinkled Amish Hands An Anthology of Amish Romance

Hannah Winstone

Published by Trellis Publishing, 2021.

This is a work of fiction. Similarities to real people, places, or events are entirely coincidental.

THESE WRINKLED AMISH HANDS AN ANTHOLOGY OF AMISH ROMANCE

First edition. June 29, 2021.

Copyright © 2021 Hannah Winstone.

ISBN: 979-8224803088

Written by Hannah Winstone.

THESE WRINKLED AMISH HANDS

HANNAH WINSTONE

Joshua Imhoff wasn't *old,* per se, but his old joints creaked in protest as he knelt beside the enormous stack of boxes in his living room. It was just one stack of many - items boxed to be thrown away or donated, but had never made it out of the front door. Most of them were filled with junk - broken ornaments or old books or things he had found in the attic while looking for something completely different.

Wrinkled hands sorted through each item methodically, patiently, picking up each one before setting it back in the box. There really *was* nothing worth keeping, and if it was up to him most of it would have been thrown away months ago, when he started this poor attempt at a 'spring' clean. It was now November.

"Joshua, what's that?" His wife, Dorcas, hovered by the door with a frown across her slender features.

Heaving a sigh, Joshua forced a smile onto his lips. "Just going through some old boxes," he replied softly, "I told you this on Tuesday."

Of course, Dorcas didn't remember that. Her memory had always been poor, but in the last few years it had plummeted to the point she hardly remembered what she had eaten for lunch. He helped as much as he could, but without modern appliances like phones or cars, even going to the Doctor's for her prescription medication was a trial.

Dorcas hovered by the door for a minute longer, her dark eyes fixed on the box like it held some fantastic secret. In reality it was just books and a handful of nick-knacks.

"These need to be thrown away," Joshua continued, even though he knew where this conversation was going to go. They had already had it once this week. "The books can be donated to charity, and I think my sister might appreciate-"

"No."

Of course. Once their home had been sweet; a little cluttered, but always clean and respectable. Over the years it had gotten worse, with Dorcas' failing health and Joshua's struggling with work and caring for his wife. Now it was at the point where she didn't want anything to be discarded at all - not even their weekly newspaper, which was almost useless once it was read.

"The house is a mess," Joshua stated calmly, even as his stomach twisted, "and it won't get better unless we make it happen. Just *one box* for now. That isn't much, is it?"

"Let me see." Carefully, Dorcas knelt beside him. Despite her failing health her joints remained as spry as a teenager's, unlike his own popping and creaking knees. She reached out to grab the first thing she saw - an old book, one neither of them had ever gotten around to finishing. "These are perfectly good books," she stated, "we can't toss these away!"

"Will you ever read it?"

"I might do," Dorcas replied with a nod. "What if we throw it away, and then I decide I want it after all?"

He pursed his lips against the sigh that threatened to break through. She said that about *everything,* even the broken lamp last week and the shattered vase the week before. Impatience simmered just beneath his skin but Joshua shoved it down, refused to let it take over. Dorcas was *sick,* and he knew that; but it didn't make it any easier to deal with.

"And this!" Dorcas exclaimed with a shriek, "we can't throw away *this.* It was the first book you ever bought me. For my twenty-fourth birthday, remember?"

Joshua let his gaze fall to the book - it was almost forty years old, wrinkled and torn through so many reads. His resolve softened, and that's when he knew Dorcas had won. The book was barely readable, but the brightness in her eyes - the kind of brightness that only rose when she remember the long past - brought a smile to his lips. "All right," he relented, "we can keep this box; but we *need* to start tidying someday."

"Yes, yes," Dorcas replied - but her attention, as short as it was, had already dissolved. She stood, clutching both books in her hands, and wandered from the room.

It was pointless trying to argue, and most days he didn't even *try;* but he couldn't humour her every time. With a sigh, Joshua packed up the box and tucked it away in a corner - a corner which was already crammed with boxes exactly like it. Another day, maybe.

Hadn't he been saying that for the last four months? Longer, even. Sometimes he wondered if his own memory was failing, what with the way the days ran together. At least he had work to keep him occupied - but more often than not he made himself sick with worry all day, thinking about Dorcas alone in the house.

He had, briefly, considered if a home might have been best for her. Somewhere with trained nurses and modern technology to keep her safe. But no, Dorcas loved their way of life, loved her neighbourhood, and he couldn't rip that away from her. Couldn't force her into somewhere so modern and unknown and then *abandon her.* So here they remained, in this tiny and cramped house, with only each other for company.

Joshua glared at the box as he hauled himself to his feet, brushed dark grey hair from his eyes. Maybe things would get easier - new neighbours were moving in today, and perhaps it would do them both good to say hello, to get out for once. It was a quiet street, mostly people who worked long hours or kept to themselves. Maybe new neighbours were exactly what they needed to change things for the better.

Speaking of *neighbours,* voices rose from the street outside. It was as if just thinking about them had summoned them into existence. The moving trucks had come the day before, but Joshua hadn't managed to catch a glimpse of the people inside. He peeked through the curtains - which were drawn for privacy - just in time to see a tall, slender woman hop out from a black car.

So they clearly weren't Amish like himself. Nothing unusual there - although this town had a high Amish population it wasn't entirely so. what *was* strange was the way the woman held herself. Stiffly, fists clenched as if steaming with anger. Then a man popped out from the driver's side and he understood.

They were arguing. Loudly, too.

The man shouted something and slammed the car door with enough force that Joshua felt the resounding *thud* even from across the street. Then he snatched the keys from the woman's hand and disappeared inside. The front door to the house shuddered as he crashed closed behind him.

"What *is* all that noise?" Dorcas demanded. At some point she had appeared behind him, glaring over his shoulder at the two newcomers with enough vehemence to make even *him* wince.

"Don't you worry," he assured quietly.

A pat on the shoulder and a quick kiss to her slender cheek calmed her down, and soon enough she was placated enough to settle into her favourite armchair - with one of the books looted from the boxes in the corner. Well, at least they were getting used.

"I'm going to see if I can help," Joshua murmured as he passed her. For a moment he thought she would come along - but she just hummed quietly in agreement. His stomach sank, but he resisted the urge to comment as he grabbed his coat. Dorcas hated leaving the house just as much as he hated leaving *her* - but forcing her to go along would only upset her.

Outside, the cold winter air hit him. No frost lay on the ground and the sky was clear, but it still made his joints ache. Not even sixty-five yet and he felt like an old man. He would be of retiring age soon, but he felt so much older. Shaking his head, Joshua hurried across the street.

The woman stood by her car, staring wistfully at the closed door, as if she wanted to go inside but couldn't *quite* bring herself to do it.

She started when Joshua waved - whether by his unusually anti-modern attire or just his sudden presence, he wasn't sue. "Sorry to bother you," he said, "but you look like you could use some help." He came to a stop beside her, and a quick glance inside the car confirmed they hadn't moved in *everything* just yet. "My name's Joshua, by the way. Joshua Imhoff."

"Oh," she replied, blinking, "Lovina Byrne."

Joshua gave her what he hoped was a reassuring smile. "You must be the new neighbour moving in? Lovely to meet you." Then, tentatively, "I couldn't help but notice your husband's raised voice. Is everything okay?"

"Boyfriend," Lovina corrected, eyes dancing downward. She fidgeted, puffing out cold air and nuzzling into her thick scarf. "He's fine, just... stressed. He gets like this when things don't go his way." Lovina shrugged then, and forced a smile that while radiant, was completely unnatural. Forced. Joshua's heart went out to her. "You must think so poorly of us, if we've made this kind of first impression." Her smile dampened.

Joshua jumped forward, ignoring the way his joints creaked, hasty to reassure. "Oh, not at all. Everyone argues - my wife and I most of all, I think. I don't think poorly of you at all.

"Wife?" Lovina asked curiously.

"Dorcas. She's inside. She... isn't up for visiting, I'm afraid."

"Oh." Lovina frowned, lips pursed. "I would invite you in, but I don't think Zach would appreciate it. He'll need time to cool off."

It was none of his business, not at all - but Joshua found himself wanting to ask just why Zach was so angry. Was he really so lonely that he was willing to pry into strangers' private lives? He huffed out a laugh at himself, raspy in the cold air, and said, "don't you worry about me - take care of yourself. Not that I need to give you advice, but perhaps you should talk to him."

"I would, if it ever worked," Lovisa replied with a huff. Cold air puffed out from her lips and she scowled at it. Then her eyes snapped wide, a small gasp leaving her lips. "I'm sorry! I shouldn't be unloading all of this on you. You don't want to hear about my troubles." She laughed but it was weak, uneasy.

Truth be told, Joshua didn't mind at all - it was someone to talk to. If there was just the slightest chance he could ease someone else's worries, it helped take his mind off of his *own*. He said as much, giving her a soft smile as he said, "it's no problem, really. The neighbours around here keep to themselves, so it's nice to have a friendly face."

"Well..." Lovisa pursed her lips, smiling shyly, "once Zach and I are settled in, perhaps you and your wife would like to visit? I won't promise a fancy dinner party or anything, but coffee and a chat is always welcome."

Joshua smiled and nodded. "Why not? Sounds lovely." Maybe he would convince Dorcas to come along. It *was* only across the road.

Just then the door cracked open and a tall, looming figure filled the doorway. "Lovina? Stop lurking outside and help unpack." Dak eyes turned to Joshua, a brow quirked - and then the man flushed, ducking his head in apology. "Sorry, I didn't realise someone else was here. Shit, why didn't you invite him in?"

"Because *you* were being childish again," Lovina sighed. There was no anger in her quiet voice, but she rolled her eyes.

The man - Zach, he knew now - glared.

Ah, time for Joshua to leave. He backed down the driveway with an apologetic smile and said, "I'll take my leave now. Take care, both of you."

Lovina watched him go - and by the time Joshua had reached his own front door their bickering resumed.

————————————

It was a week before Joshua saw the neighbours again. Between work and Dorcas there wasn't much time for anything else; and the spare time he *did* have was spent trying futilely to clean up around the house. In all honesty he had completely forgotten until a week later on his way back from Church.

The next day he made a point of cooking something special, something a little more indulgent than he was used to, and boxing it up for the newcomers. If anything he thought Lovina would appreciate it - Zach... well, he would see.

"I'm just going around to see the new neighbours," Joshua spoke as he tucked the meal under his arms, "would you like to come with me?"

Unsurprisingly, Dorcas shook her head. "I'm busy," she snapped. In reality she had been staring at the same page of her knitting magazine for twenty minutes, the mug of tea beside her long cold. Still, her eyes skimmed over the paragraphs with practised focus as her slender hands fidgeted in her lap.

Joshua could have pushed the matter, but what good would that do? He pressed a kiss to the top of her head and replied, "I'll be back soon. You know where to find me if you need."

But Dorcas' attention had already drifted from him. She turned the page in her magazine, eyes fluttering across words she wasn't *really* reading.

With one last longing look, Joshua stepped outside. He hurried across the road, skin already flushing pink from the cold, ignoring the way his aching joints protested at his speed. At least the meal, still tucked safely underneath his arm, was still radiating heat. He knocked on the door and waited.

A beaming face met his, Bright blue eyes widened in recognition, and Lovina darted aside to let him in. "Joshua, hi!" Her smile, with a little gap between her two front teeth, reminded him of Dorcas in her youth - of course, Lovina's loose floral shirt and oversized jacket wasn't like Dorcas at all. Perhaps, if he and Dorcas had ever had children, they might have turned out like Lovina.

Shaking his head to dispel the thoughts, Joshua stepped inside. The warmth hit him immediately - as did the steady beat of music from a room upstairs. Although it was muffled by the door, it didn't conceal the overbearing vocals *or* the heavy guitar.

"Sorry," Lovina muttered, "Zach's been listening to music *all day* and I can't get him to shut it off. Sometimes I think he listens to it just so he won't have to talk to me. Anyway," her eyes widened, broad smile returning, "how have you been? I haven't seen you since that first day."

"I was planning to bring you a housewarming gift, but I've been busy," he admitted with a shrug, "I thought, since you haven't finished unpacking, that a few hot meals would do you good."

Lovina simply *beamed* as he offered her the food he had prepared. Dorcas had helped, eager to get involved in a rare show of eagerness. Inside was a heavy dish filled with a chicken and dumpling casserole, along with fresh baked bread and maple syrup cookies. Lovina grinned as she caught sight of the cookies. "Oh, thank you! This all looks delicious."

"I'm sure it's boring compared to what you're used to," Joshua replied with a lighthearted laugh as she led him to the kitchen. The kitchen itself was a mess of half opened boxes and kitchen utensils. It reminded him of his *own* house. He perched on a stool and watched idly as Lovina fetched mugs - from inside a box marked *dishes.*

"It looks lovely," Lovina assured, "do you take sugar and milk?"

"Just milk," Joshua replied.

As Lovina set about making coffee, Joshua let his mind wander to upstairs. Had Zach left Lovina to unpack everything? He couldn't imagine someone being so inconsiderate - but then again, he had only met the man briefly. So briefly it barely even counted. "I don't mean to pry," Joshua spoke without even realising he had opened his mouth, "but you and Zach - why did you move here?"

"Oh." Lovina paused with the mugs in her hand, lips tilting into a frown. "Well, we come from the city - but I grew up in a small town, and the city was just too loud, you know? I needed a break from it all."

"If you wanted a break, you could have just taken a trip, not moved all the way here."

Lovina laughed, sloshing a drop of coffee onto the table as she set down the mugs. "I know, but I never liked city life. This is much more... *me.*" She sighed then, taking a sip of coffee as if mulling over her next words. Then, "Zach agreed to it, but I don't think its what he wanted. He just... never *tells me* these things. Expects me to just read his mind and understand."

Joshua stared into his own coffee, as if it held all the answers.

"But you don't want to hear about that-"

"I do," Joshua interrupted, smiling gently, "you clearly need to talk about it with *someone,* and I can't imagine you know many folks here yet."

"True..." Lovina trailed off.

"If I'm being truthful here; it's nice to talk to someone, get out for once. My wife and I... outside of each other, we don't see many people. She's sick, so I have to stay home and look after her."

"Oh." Lovina frowned, sympathy washing over her thin features. "I had no idea, I'm sorry."

"Don't be," Joshua replied honestly, "all I meant was that I don't mind if you need to unload. Everyone does, sometimes. Maybe you just need to have an honest sit down chat with Zach, make him see from your point of view. Tell me how it goes, afterword."

For a moment she paused, head tilted in thought. Then she beamed, nodding enthusiastically. "I'll do that. Now, would you like to share these *delicious* looking maple cookies with me?"

The rest of the afternoon went much easier after that, and Joshua went home feeling lighter than he had in a long time.

———————————

Joshua sat with a book in his hands, Dorcas silently sipping tea beside him. Soft classical music played through their ancient radio, and the house must have been the most peaceful it had been in *years*.

Until a deep, hollering voice shot through the slightly open window.

Dorcas bolted to her feet, tea spilling onto the carpet, and whirled to face the window. "Who's shouting at this time in the morning?"

"It's after midday, love," Joshua replied patiently. He turned to coax her back onto the sofa, arm outstretched, but she continued to glare through her glasses and the window to the street outside. Sighing, Joshua hauled himself upright. "Dorcas, what is it?"

"Those neighbours are screaming at each other again," she huffed, "Look."

Sure enough, Lovina stood in the doorway calling after Zach - who had already marched half way down the street to the end of the cul-de-sac. Lovina folded thin arms across her chest, staring after Zach with furrowed brows.

At the sight, even Dorcas softened. "We should invite her in," she suggested quietly, "she looks lonely."

Joshua looked across the room, at the multitude of boxes and dusty bookcases and scores of old newspapers. He squirmed at the thought of letting someone see this mess - but he hated to think Lovina was going back to an empty house. Relenting, he went to the door.

Lovina hadn't budged, and her head snapped up when she caught sight of him standing on his porch. "I'm sorry," she called across the street, "I hope we didn't disturb you!"

Instead of replying, Joshua called her over. "Come inside. I have streusel cake and tea - and I think it's about time you met my wife."

Lovina managed a small smile as she climbed the porch steps. "I'd hate to intrude," she murmured - but Joshua was already ushering her inside. She relaxed into the warmth, courtesy of the small wood burning stove in their living room, and shucked off her boots. "Thanks. You must think we do nothing but fight." She laughed quietly.

"Did you talk to him?"

Shrugging, she avoided her gaze. That was a no, then. "I've been busy, and every time I've tried something else got in the way. I suppose by now I'm just making excuses."

Joshua smiled kindly, gesturing to the kitchen. "Maybe a hot drink will do you good. You can always talk to him another day, once he's calmed down."

The two meandered to the kitchen, and Dorcas made her appearance a moment later. She smiled - and she seemed so genuinely *delighted* to meet someone new. Dorcas hadn't been interested in meeting new people in years. That in itself was a wonder. Even more so was the way she plopped down at the table beside her, and stuck out a hand to shake. "Hello, dear. I'm Dorcas. You are...?"

"Lovina," she replied with a smile. They shook hands, and Lovina beamed. They really *did* look alike, Dorcas and Lovina. If they were the same age, they could have been sisters. Twins, even.

They chatted while Joshua made tea, although he didn't do much talking himself. It was so *unusual* to see Dorcas hold a conversation, let alone with a stranger. Warmth spread through Joshua's chest as he listened, a smile creeping across his features as Dorcas giggled like a teenager.

He almost forgot he was pouring tea, until his elbow knocked a stack of clean dishes and the tea splashed against the kitchen counter. He hopped back with a hiss, narrowly avoiding the scalding liquid.

"Are you all right?" Lovina jumped to her feet while Dorcas looked on, blinking in confusion.

"Fine, yes," Joshua replied with an embarrassed flush. It was only a matter of time until something like this happened. The entire house was so full of *junk* and there was barely an inch of counter space free. Sighing, he set down the teapot and fetched a towel.

Lovina hovered, mopping up the spill alongside him. "Why don't you put those dishes away and I'll finish this?" she asked brightly.

Joshua flushed darker. He felt like a senile old man, incapable of caring for his own home. "There's no space in the cupboard," he admitted with a shrug, "these ones are all chipped, ready to be discarded?"

"Then why don't you throw them away?"

He shifted, tossing the towel to the side to be washed later. He was being *scrutinised,* wasn't he? Judged. "I can't. Dorcas creates a fuss whenever I try and I've just... never gotten around to it."

He half expected Lovina to scoff, to call him ridiculous. He *also* expected Dorcas to protest, to blame it on him as she often did. Neither of those things happened.

Instead Lovina tapped a finger to her chin, deep in thought. Then, "how about I make a deal with you?"

"A *deal?*" he repeated incredulously. What ever could she mean by that.

Lovina picked up a mug for Dorcas, setting it down on the table before fetching her own. "If I talk to Zach and make up with him, will you try to tidy up? Just one room. I can swing by, help you with it."

"But Dorcas-"

"I need to stop making excuses not to sort things with Zach. Maybe *you* need to stop making excuses not to fix the house." She quirked a brow, daring him to disagree. Then she threw out a hand.

Honestly, she was *right.* Dorcas hated him throwing anything away but it needed to be done - was he just using his wife as an excuse to let things continue? Maybe.

"All right, I agree." Sighing, Joshua held out his own hand, and they shook on it.

"Great. I'll be here tomorrow at three."

———————————

Three o'clock rolled around the next day - and then passed just as quickly. By the time half-past three arrived Joshua was beginning to think Lovina had forgotten. He had even started on the enormous stack of boxes in the living room by himself - and Dorcas had none of her usual protests.

It was nearly four in the afternoon by the time the doorbell rang - and Joshua shot up from his seat with such speed it left his knees aching. Yet he made his way slowly to the door, unwilling to appear too overeager even as a smile spread across his lined face.

Lovina stood outside, bundled up in a massive coat. Joshua stood aside to let her in - and then paused when he caught sight of the enormous figure behind her. "I hope you don't mind, I brought Zach along," Lovina chirped, "he doesn't start his new job until next week and, well, we both want to help."

Zach gave him an awkward nod, thick hair falling across his shoulders. He had a dark sort of look, something he had heard people refer to as *punk*. Nothing like Lovina's bright, floral look. Still he smiled, almost shyly, and sidled inside along with Lovina.

"It's no trouble," Joshua replied with a smile, "come in. Would either of you like a drink?"

"Coffee, please! I can help you make it. Hey Zach, why don't you introduce yourself to Dorcas?"

He held her gaze for a moment - as if to protest - but then he nodded and made his way into the living room. Joshua almost protested, nerves gripping him. He should be there when they met, just in case Dorcas caused a fuss-

"They'll be fine," Lovina whispered, a smile gracing her lips, "Zach's not as scary as he looks. Let's go make those drinks."

Honestly, he doubted it - he had seen the way he shouted at Lovina, hated to think of him getting angry with Dorcas - but Lovina's bright grin was enough to convince him, at least for now. He followed Lovina into the kitchen, taking out four mugs. Silence descended as they worked, but it didn't feel thick and awkward. It was... *nice.*

Then Lovina sidled up beside him, gesturing with one hand to the living room beyond. "I spoke to Zach, like you suggested," she began amicably, "and you were right."

"About what?" He reached for the tea, nestled among the clutter.

"About me needing to stand my ground, about needing to communicate. Everything, really."

Joshua couldn't help but smile. Good. Someone as sweet as her deserved only the best. A swell of fatherly protectiveness rose inside him and he physically stepped back. Oh. That was new.

If Lovina noticed, she thankfully didn't let on. "I'm not saying everything's fixed between us, but I think we're getting there. He's came with me today, which is more than I'd have expected two weeks ago."

Setting the kettle on the stove to boil, he turned to her. "I'm glad you worked things out. I'll admit, I wasn't sure it would work. Not that I don't have any faith in you-"

"I know," Lovina replied with a laugh, "Zach's got his issues, but I *do* love him. And he moved across the state with me, changed up his entire life - so I guess he loves me too."

"Of course he does."

Silence fell upon them again, broken only by the whistle of the kettle as it boiled. Joshua didn't need to say anything more - Lovina was happy, and his advice had worked, so what else mattered? It seemed that in only a handful of weeks they had changed each other's lives without even meaning to. Not that he was complaining - quite the opposite.

By the time the tea was ready, soft voices had risen from the living room. A soft, girlish giggle followed by a much less delicate snort of laughter.

"Zach's *laughing?*," Lovina joked, "he must be enjoying himself."

The two beelined for the living room - only to stop dead at the sight before them. Dorcas sat on her favourite spot by the fireplace, a black photo album in her hands. Zach perched beside her, holding in laughter as she told him the story behind one particular photograph.

"I didn't realise we still had that album," Joshua muttered. He set down the mugs and wandered over, smile tugging at his features. "Dorcas love, where did you find that?"

"Bookshelf," she replied with a grin, "stuck behind those old novels of yours. We really need to get rid of some of that junk."

Joshua groaned, dropping his head in his hands. He'd been telling her that for *years*. Still, warmth bloomed in his chest, threatening to spill over as he pressed a kiss to her forehead. "We do," he replied simply, "so why don't we start now?"

"Lovina and I are here to help," Zach spoke - and his voice was oddly soft, softer than Joshua had ever heard it. Then again, he had only ever heard the man shout and yell until now. He stepped back, arm looped around Lovina's waist, and regarded the room. "Where do you want to start?"

"Well, the boxes are already out so it makes sense to start there..." Joshua flushed, "it is a terrible mess. I'm sorry."

Lovina beamed. "Don't be! That's why we're here. So grab a box and lets start."

The four of them settled down with their drinks, chatting idly as they sorted through box after box. By the end of that day, the living room was sparkling clean, not a single piece of junk or dust in sight. It was better than it had ever looked, and Joshua had lived there since he was twenty-nine.

When it was time for them to say goodbye, there was a lightness in his chest that he hadn't felt in years.

———————————

The weeks fell into a routine, after that. After work, they alternated between spending the evening at Joshua's or helping Lovina and Zach unpack. By the end of the month both of their houses were spotless, almost perfect. Not a single box remained in either home.

So, Joshua decided to celebrate. It had been years since he had hosted guests and he was out of practice, but they had all agreed to have dinner at his that Friday evening. He and Dorcas dressed in their best clothes - which were still plain in comparison to modern outfits - and set the table with their best china.

The scent of hot food filled the house as he and Dorcas cooked side by side, music drifting from their old radio. He couldn't remember the last time Dorcas had really taken an interest in anything, and it was so wonderful to see her eagerly hum along to the music as she kneaded the bread dough with steady hands.

Joshua wasn't even sure what people like Lovina and Jack *liked* to eat, but he remembered her delight at those maple cookies and decided that was somewhere to start.

"When are they arriving again?"

Joshua blinked, brought from his thoughts by Dorcas' soft voice. He had told her three times since they awoke that morning - but the fact she remembered they were having guests at all was a warming surprise. "Seven o'clock love," he reminded gently.

Dorcas hummed and nodded, eyes focused on the dough in her slender hands. "That young man - Zach - doesn't he remind you of Matthew?"

Matthew. Dorcas' brother, although they hadn't seen each other in a long time. The question left him stunned, frozen with a knife half way to the cutting board. "You never speak about Matthew," he replied quietly.

Dorcas hummed along to the music, completely unaware of how *odd* her question was. After a moment she stopped kneading and turned to him with an abruptness that left him speechless. "We know his address," Dorcas replied, "we should visit him sometime." And then she went back to baking as if nothing had happened.

Joshua floundered, lips parting even though no sound came out. She remembered Matthew's address? The address of a man she hadn't even spoken of in almost a decade? Half the time she couldn't remember what had happened an hour ago. He pursed his lips, staring down at the half chopped vegetables as if *they* somehow held the answers.

Had Lovina - and by extension, Zach - really been such a wonderful influence on her? If so, he had a lot more to thank them for than he imagined. Just seeing Dorcas, so bright and cheerful in a way he had thought was gone forever, warmed his heart.

"Hurry up, or we won't be ready in time," Dorcas huffed - but she smiled too.

Smiling back, Joshua resumed his methodical chopping. There would be time to reminisce later - but perhaps not when he was holding an enormous kitchen knife.

Soon enough everything was ready, and all they had to do was wait. The bread cooled on the counter top, the winter stew was in the oven, and the cookies were almost done. The sweet scent of the cookies mingled with the savoury of the stew and blanketed everything in a soft, cosy feel. Joshua hadn't realised how much he *missed* feeling like this. It almost felt like Christmas, even with over two months to go.

Speaking of Christmas, it was as if Dorcas had read his mind. She settled into her armchair by the fire, holding a steaming cup of coffee in her hands. "Do you think Lovina might like to spend Christmas with us? I don't know if they even celebrate..."

Joshua, hiding a smile behind his hand, replied, "I'm sure they would love to. We can ask this evening over dinner."

Christmas had always been a small affair for them - and since they celebrated on January sixth instead of the more common December twenty-fifth, there hadn't been many people to share it with. Until

Lovina and Zach arrived it had always just been the two of them. Even when members of their Church had asked them to join, Dorcas had always been unwilling to attend. He supposed this was just another thing that had changed - and changed for the *better*.

Joshua settled down on the chair opposite Dorcas, enjoying the crackle of the fire as it warmed his hands. "We could always celebrate twice this year," he mused, "December with Lovina and Zach-"

"And in January, just us two," Dorcas finished with a nod of approval that made Joshua laugh. "I think that sounds lovely."

Joshua opened his mouth to reply - only to be cut short as the doorbell rang, piercing his ears with a jolt. A moment later a cheerful voice, muffled, called, "it's us!"

Joshua and Dorcas shared a smile, warmth spreading through his chest, before Joshua stood to answer. "They're early," he mused - although there was cheer in his voice.

"Better than being late," Dorcas replied softly.

Nodding in agreement, he went to fetch them.

Lovina and Zach stood huddled on the porch. Johua hadn't even *known* it was snowing but a thick, fluffy layer of white surrounded them. Lovina's nose was tinged pink, while Zach's entire face was scarlet with the cold.

He ushered them inside, huffing against the icy cold, and helped Lovina struggle out of her enormous coat. "Did you know it was snowing?" he called to Dorcas.

"No!" she gasped back - and within *seconds* she was in the hallway, nose pressed against the glass. Lovina chuckled, but Dorcas was too busy gazing at the pristine white snow outside.

Dorcas had always claimed snow brought good luck - she *also* claimed that her favourite memories took place in the snow, and they were some of the only memories she had held onto as her illness progressed. Perhaps it was a good sign, then. A sign that the future was bright for them, or a sigh that they had finally overcome their obstacles.

Either way, Joshua knew that it wasn't *snow* that decided that for them, whether his wife claimed it was a good omen or not. They decided it for themselves - and as long as the four of them remained friends, he didn't doubt things would be just fine.

A LEAP OF FAITH

STEPHANIE SWIFT

Hope Miller laced her fingers together on top of her lap and did her best to empty her mind so she could focus on Bishop Abram's sermon.

It wasn't an easy task.

Sitting to her right was her mother and father, both of whom sat with rigid backs and facial expressions as hard and stern as the wooden pew they were seated on. To her left were her aunt Martha and uncle Seth, who both appeared comfortable and at ease, holding hands and smiling as they listened to the message. The two couples couldn't be more opposite if they tried, and she felt like neutral ground between them, which was disconcerting to say the least.

Hope cautiously looked over her right shoulder and smiled at Noah Wyse, her closest friend and ally. He sat a couple of pews behind them on the other side of the sanctuary with his six-year-old daughter, Ivy, who gave her a shy wave when she caught Hope looking their way. She wanted to wave back at her, but she knew if her mother or father caught her goofing off during the service she would never hear the end of it.

Noah gave her a sympathetic smile, and she turned her attention back to Bishop Abram before she made the mistake of smiling back at him and causing an uproar if one of the elders of the church caught her doing it. Even though she and Noah were just friends, it was highly frowned upon in their small Amish community for the unmarried men and women to cavort with each other unless they were promised to marry. It was ridiculous, really, but the last thing she wanted to do was cause a scene.

Hope sighed. If only things were simpler and less complicated. At twenty years old, she was one of the oldest from her generation who hadn't married, but that didn't bother her in the least. After growing up in a home with parents who shared a loveless marriage, a relationship was the furthest thing from her mind. Because of their strict faith, divorce was next to impossible, but there were many times during her youth when she wished her parents would go their separate ways. She couldn't imagine what brought the two of them together, unless it was an arranged courtship, because there was no way to picture them ever being in love.

Her aunt and uncle, on the other hand, were the epitome of love and devotion. You could see it in the way they looked at each other that their love was real. When Hope made the decision to leave home three years prior and move in with her aunt and uncle to help with her quilting business, the relief she felt was overwhelming. Gone were the days stepping on egg shells around her parents and living in a home that was so cold she could feel it in her bones. With Hope being their only child, she could only imagine how depressing the atmosphere must be now that they were alone together, and the thought made her heart ache.

No, she would never get married. Not if it meant she would lose a piece of herself and spend the rest of her days wishing for her freedom. No man was worth that.

Her mother nudged her side, startling her and making her jump. She hadn't realized she'd drifted off into her own little world, but the service was nearly over and every head in the room was bowed as Bishop Abram said his closing prayer. Hope shut her eyes as her cheeks burned hot from embarrassment. As soon as the Bishop said "amen", and everyone started for the door, her mother was on her case.

"Honestly, Hope...do you ever stop daydreaming?" she muttered.

Hope took a deep breath to keep from saying something she regretted. "I'm sorry, mother."

As they stood in line for the door, she glanced around the room in search of Noah and Ivy, but didn't find them. Hope peered through one of the church windows to see if they had already left the church, and she spotted them near a grove of trees with Victoria Kaufmann, a young widow from their area. While Noah and Victoria talked, Ivy played close by on a tire swing hanging from an old oak tree.

The two of them were deep in conversation about something, and when Victoria reached out and touched Noah's arm, Hope's temper bristled in response, which caught her off guard. *What was that about?* she wondered. She and Noah had never been romantically involved, and it wasn't the first time a single woman had flirted with Noah since his wife, Maria, passed away not long after Ivy was born.

"Are you alright?"

Hope looked behind her at her aunt Sadie, who was eyeing her skeptically. "*Yah*. Why do you ask?"

Sadie shrugged and smiled. "You just seemed puzzled for some reason."

Puzzled was putting it lightly, but Hope shook her head to clear her thoughts and to keep from dwelling on it. She and Noah were just friends, and it was probably just her over-protectiveness getting the best of her anyway. She knew very well how desperate some of her single friends were when it came to marriage, and she didn't want to see Noah hurt. That was all. He and Ivy had been through enough.

When they finally made their way outside, Hope and her aunt and uncle followed her parents to their horse and carriage to see them off, and Hope forced herself not to look in Noah and Victoria's direction.

"Sister, we would love for you and William to join us for lunch."

Hope rolled her eyes heavenward. It was the same thing every Sunday, and it always ended the same way - with her parents refusing. She would never understand how her aunt Sadie could be so patient with them when they treated her so callously.

Her mother and father stopped walking and turned to look at them. Her lips were pursed and her roughly chiseled face was set in her usual sour expression. Her father's face held no expression whatsoever.

"*Denki*, Sadie, but I'm afraid we'll have to decline. Hope, may I speak to you in private?"

Hope inhaled sharply and glimpsed at her aunt Sadie, who appeared just as perplexed. It was odd for her mother to want to talk to her about anything, much less alone. When she grabbed Hope's elbow and roughly led her a few feet away, she held her breath, expecting the worst.

"When are you coming home?" her mother asked.

Hope furrowed a brow as she pulled away from her mother's grasp. "What do you mean? I don't plan on moving back home. We've already discussed this."

Her mother huffed and puffed as she crossed her arms haughtily over her chest. "You need to stop being a burden to your aunt and uncle."

Hope took a step back. Her mother was never one to mince words, but her accusation stung. She looked over at her aunt and uncle, who were unsuccessfully trying to pull her father into conversation.

"I'm not a burden to them. How can you say that?"

Her mother wouldn't be swayed. "You're an adult, and you can't live with them forever. It's time for you to grow up and find a husband while there's still time."

Hope blinked twice. "While there's still time? You mean, while I'm still young enough to snag one?"

She didn't want to be disrespectful, but this time her mother was close to crossing the line. There was a significant difference between being concerned and acting downright rude. She hated to consider that she might be right. Did her aunt Martha and uncle Seth really consider her a burden? They'd never said anything about her overstaying her welcome, but perhaps they were just being nice.

Hope felt her eyes sting with hot tears, but she blinked them back, refusing to let her mother see that she'd gotten under her skin. Fortunately, she turned and walked back to the group before Hope had the chance to say anything further, which was probably for the best. The last place she wanted to fight with her was in the church yard with the whole congregation listening in.

She cast a wayward glance in Noah's direction, but he was still busy talking to Victoria Kaufmann and oblivious to everything else. Ivy noticed her right away and gave her a big wave as she swung back and forth on the tire swing with a silly grin highlighting her beautiful little face. Hope waved back before resigning herself to return to her family.

* * * *

Noah leaned slightly to his left so he could peek over Victoria's shoulder, and he felt his blood boil when he saw Hope talking to her mother. Actually, her mother was doing most of the talking, and he could tell from the sullen look on her face that the woman wasn't happy...as usual.

"Noah? Is something wrong?"

Her turned his attention back to Victoria, feeling guilty that he'd let his thoughts roam elsewhere. Victoria was a sweet woman, and even though he had no interest in anything other than friendship, it was obvious she felt differently. It may have been a long time since he was with another woman, but he knew flirting when he saw it.

"I'm so sorry. What were you saying?" he asked.

Victoria touched his arm again, something he noticed she was doing quite frequently while they talked. Any other man may have enjoyed it, but he'd already been blessed with the love of his life, and he wouldn't risk his heart being broken again. Plus, there was his daughter to think about, and he was far more concerned with her well-being than anything else.

"I asked if you were planning on attending the charity auction this Saturday. I'll be donating a picnic lunch."

So that was what she was getting at. It was all perfectly clear now. The auction was being held to raise money toward new books and other materials for their community schoolhouse, and it was tradition for the single women to make picnic lunches to be auctioned off among the single men. The winner would then share the lunch with the woman who donated it.

"*Yah*, I hope I can. It just depends on if I get my orders finished in time."

It wasn't a lie. Being the only blacksmith in the area, there was seldom a weekend that passed where he wasn't busy working overtime to finish orders. Not only did he have orders to complete for his neighbors, but several shop owners in nearby Lancaster were faithful customers too.

"Well, perhaps I'll see you there," she replied.

She gave him a shy smile before she turned and walked away, and Noah expelled a long breath. He stole a glance at Ivy as she played on the tire swing, and his heart swelled twice its size when she grinned back at him. She favored her mother so much it was hard not to look at her without feeling a deep pang in his chest.

He ached for the things she was missing out on not having her mother in her life. It wouldn't be long before she was a teenager, and even though he did his best to tend to her every need, there was a special bond a mother and daughter shared that he could never fill and he knew that. Ivy needed a woman in her life, and even though he missed the closeness and companionship a relationship provided, he just couldn't bear the thought of taking such a huge risk.

Noah caught sight of Hope and her aunt and uncle as he steered their horse and wagon out of the church yard and right on the main road, headed for home. Hope sat on the far right of the seat with her hands clasped together on her lap, staring off into the distance. Of all the women he knew, she was the only one he considered a close friend he could talk to and rely on. He'd bent her ear many times since Maria's passing, and she'd been there for Ivy more times than he could count.

If only they were on the same path. It wasn't as if he'd never considered the two of them as a couple, because he had many times, but Hope's parents made her jaded to the whole concept of love and marriage. Noah, on the other hand, knew the depths of love and what he stood to lose if he went down that road again, and it frightened him more than he cared to admit.

"Are you ready to go, daddy?"

Ivy appeared by his side, and when she placed her small hand in his, he forced the troubling thoughts from his mind and smiled at her. She needed him more than anyone else in his life now, and that was all that mattered. Everything else would have to wait.

* * * *

"I can't believe I'm doing this," Hope remarked.

She grimaced when she saw her friends standing in line at the auction, each of them appearing anxious as they waited to turn over their picnic baskets to Bishop Abram, who was serving as the auctioneer for the event. They were all clothed in what looked like brand-new dresses and bonnets, and they looked excited - giddy even.

"Oh, stop. It's all for a worthy cause. Did I ever tell you this is how your uncle Seth and I met?'

Hope looked beside her at her aunt Sadie, and she attempted a smile but failed miserably. If it hadn't been for her aunt's incessant nagging, she never would have agreed to taking part in such a silly tradition, but she'd come too far to back out now.

"Just look at those single men over there staring at you. I think they're memorizing what your basket looks like so they can bid on it."

Her aunt giggled as she said it, but when Hope saw the gentlemen she was referring to, her heart sank. There was Gabriel, one of the most conceited men in town, who thought he was God's gift to women, and there was Amos, a man three years younger than her who was at least a foot shorter than her too.

There were several other men in the group, but she didn't know most of them. She noticed Noah standing a few feet away, but she doubted he would take part in any of the festivities since he never had before. She'd managed to get out of it over the past four years, but her aunt had such a vise-like grip on her arm, she knew running wouldn't be an option this time around.

"Aunt Sadie, can I ask you something? I want you to be completely honest with me too."

Her aunt gave her a curious look before nodding.

"Am I a burden to you and uncle Seth?"

Her aunt tightened her grip and turned her around so they were face-to-face. Hope could tell by the look in her eyes that her question upset her.

"Of course not. You've never been a burden to us. Why would you even ask such a thing? Has my sister been filling your head with nonsense again?"

Hope smiled. Her aunt Sadie could always sense when something was bothering her, especially when it had to do with her mother. The two women were like night and day and had supposedly never gotten along during their childhood. As adults they merely tolerated each other, but it wasn't as if her aunt didn't try to build a relationship between the two of them. It was her mother who refused to budge.

"We love having you with us, and there's no way I could run my quilting business without you. You've been a Godsend, and don't you dare let your mother tell you any different. Now...get over there and get in line."

She gave her a little push and Hope had no choice but to do as she said. She made her way to the end of the line, literally dragging her feet with every step. If someone like Gabriel or Amos won her basket it would be the longest picnic lunch of her life. Hopefully, someone she could at least put up with for an hour or so would bid on her basket and win.

When Hope inched her way to the front of the line and handed over her basket to Bishop Abram, he looked surprised to see her. "I'm glad you're participating this year, Hope."

She prayed her feelings weren't painfully obvious on her face because she hated to disappoint him. Not trusting herself to speak, she simply smiled at him before making her way back to her aunt Sadie.

There were several other fundraising festivities taking place, and since the auction wasn't scheduled for at least another hour, the two of them walked around admiring the assorted pies, cookies, and other goods for sale. Hope tried not to dwell on the upcoming auction and have fun, especially since social gatherings were far and few between in her little community.

"Looks like Noah will have his hands full deciding who he's going to have lunch with," Sadie said.

Hope followed her gaze to the makeshift stage where the auction was going to be held. Noah stood off to the side of the stage, where he was flanked by three women – Victoria and two other women she didn't recognize. All four of them were talking and laughing, and the women's intentions were obvious by the way they batted their eyelashes at him and stood so close to him she wondered how he could breathe.

"It looks that way," she replied.

For reasons she couldn't explain, seeing the women fawn over him made her uneasy. The thought that he might be interested in one of them brought with it the realization that although they were good friends, it probably wouldn't always be that way, especially if he remarried. After all, what woman would put up with her husband having a close friendship with another woman, no matter how innocent it might be?

"Something troubling you?"

She turned to her aunt, who was eyeing her with an amused look on her face.

"No. Why do you ask?"

Her aunt put her hands on her hips and laughed. "Really, Hope? I have a tough time believing you don't feel a tad bit jealous seeing those women flirt with Noah. You had this same look on your face at church when you saw him talking to Victoria."

Hope's jaw slacked. That was crazy. Why in the world would she be jealous? They were just friends and nothing more. He'd mentioned many times how he wasn't interested in dating again, and...well, there was no way she would risk becoming as unhappy as her mother.

Before she could redeem herself, Bishop Abram was taking the stage and ushering everyone to sit down. Several of the pews from the church had been brought outside for the auction and as Hope and Sadie sat down on the middle row, she noticed Noah making his way to the back, were he stood behind the last pew. He waved at her when he caught her staring at him, and Hope waved back quickly and turned around to face the front, hoping he didn't see her cheeks burning red from embarrassment.

As soon as everyone was seated, Bishop Abram made his way to the podium and the table beside it that was littered with more baskets than she could count. She'd considered the number of single women donating to the auction, but she'd forgotten about the handful of widows, young and old, who might be participating – including Victoria Kaufmann.

Hope searched for her in the crowd and found her sitting near the front. When Victoria turned around in her seat, there was no denying her gaze was centered on Noah as a huge smile spread across her face. Even though Hope wanted to look at him to see what his reaction was, she forced herself not to, especially since her aunt Sadie was watching her every move.

Bishop Abram welcomed everyone to the auction before picking up the first basket – a large red wicker basket that he noted was loaded to the brim with homemade goodies like chicken and dumplings and blackberry cobbler. The bidding started at five dollars, and it didn't take long for the price to climb as several men placed their bids. It eventually sold for forty dollars to an older gentleman named Aaron, who'd been a widower for many years.

When Hope saw Clara, a middle-aged widow, pick up the basket and make her way over to Aaron and sit down, she wondered if she was the only one who detected the sly grin that passed between the two of them. She had to admit it was adorable, and part of her was kind of envious of them too.

The auction continued for at least an hour before Bishop Abram finally picked up Hope's basket. There were only three remaining, and Victoria was also waiting for hers to be called. She noticed Noah hadn't placed a bid on anything, which meant he was probably waiting on

Victoria, and that bothered her more than it probably should have. Amos had, thankfully, already bid on and won a basket, so he was out of the bidding, but Gabriel hadn't, and that made her very nervous, especially when he turned and looked her way. The wink he gave her made her nauseous, and she considered running for the hills, but her aunt Sadie wouldn't hear of it.

"The winner of this basket will be treated to a fine lunch, complete with fried chicken, fresh corn on the cob, biscuits, pecan pie, and lemonade. Let's start the bidding at five dollars," Bishop Abram said.

Just as she feared, Gabriel waved his hand in the air.

"Five dollars!" Bishop Abram yelled. "Can I get ten dollars?"

A man she didn't know took the bid, but Gabriel trumped him by bidding twenty dollars. Hope started feeling sick to her stomach. *This couldn't be happening.* The two men kept going back and forth for what seemed like forever, and she could tell that Gabriel was getting annoyed.

"Who is that man?" Hope whispered, pointing to the other bidder. "I don't recognize him."

"He just moved here about a month ago," Sadie replied. "He bought the Troyer's old dairy farm."

Hope sighed. It was bad enough that she might be forced into having lunch with someone as obnoxious as Gabriel, but trying to find something to talk about with a stranger wasn't a fun option either.

"Sixty dollars!" Bishop Abram called.

Gabriel once again raised his hand, and when the Bishop asked for sixty-five, the other gentleman didn't make a move and neither did anyone else. It was the highest bid of the auction so far, which probably should have made her happy, but not under the current circumstances. Gabriel looked her way and the smug grin on his face made her stomach twist into knots.

"Sixty dollars going once, going twice..."

"One hundred dollars!"

Hope inhaled sharply, as did most of the crowd, when someone's voice boomed from the back row. She felt her heart catch in her throat. That wasn't just any voice. She would know it anywhere. Turning slowly in her seat, Hope saw Noah with his hand held high in the air. A hush fell over the crowd, and no one said anything for the longest time, including Bishop Abram, who appeared more stunned than anyone.

When he finally found his tongue again, he called for a higher bid, but no one made a motion to accept it. She glanced at Gabriel, who sat with his arms crossed over his chest and a scowl on his face.

"One hundred dollars! Going once, going twice...SOLD to Mr. Noah Wyse!"

Everyone clapped, and Bishop Abram held out her basket so she could come get it, but she felt glued to the seat. It took her aunt Sadie's prompting – or rather, *pushing* – to make her move, and when she retrieved the basket and turned to walk back, she didn't miss the look of contempt on Victoria Kaufmann's face.

Hope made her way to the back of the crowd and stood beside Noah as Bishop Abram picked up another basket she recognized as Victoria's. She wanted to say something to Noah, but she felt shy for some strange reason and so she stood beside him and waited for the auction to end. To say she was grateful Gabriel didn't win her basket would be an understatement, but Victoria wasn't so lucky. When he placed the highest bid on her basket, there was no denying the disapproving look on her face as she grabbed the basket from Bishop Abram's hands and sat down beside Gabriel on the front pew.

When the auction finally ended, Noah started walking in the direction of her aunt Sadie, which both intrigued and worried her as she followed him. When they approached, her aunt gave her another sly smile, but she rolled her eyes heavenward and chose to ignore it.

"Mrs. Sadie, do you mind if I take Hope home this afternoon?"

His question surprised her, but it didn't seem to faze her aunt, who agreed with more enthusiasm than she expected. When Sadie said

Noah put a hand up to stop her before she flew into a tirade. "I promise I wasn't trying to do anything sneaky behind your back, but I'm determined to make you see that this...*us*...would work. You've just got to have a little faith in love, Hope. Your parents might be unhappy, but that doesn't mean you're destined to be unhappy too. I would never do anything to hurt you. You should already know that about me."

She appeared to be on the verge of crying, and he felt like kicking himself. Nothing was going as he planned, but he couldn't stop now. If he didn't get his point across before it was too late, he knew he risked losing her forever – even as a friend.

Noah gently touched her cheek and let his fingertips slide over her jaw to her lips. "I'm going to kiss you now," he murmured, softly. "Afterwards, if you can honestly tell me you felt nothing at all, then I promise I will let this go, and we'll never speak of it again."

Her eyes widened and she looked terrified, but he noticed she didn't shy away from his touch or try to stop him either. "Noah, no...I've never..."

He smiled as he tenderly cradled her head in his hands, "I know. You've just got to trust me."

When he leaned in close and pressed his lips against her own, he could tell right away how nervous she was by the way her lips quivered, but the effect she had on him was undeniable. His body burned hot with desire, and he felt the insatiable urge to take her in his arms, but he also didn't want to frighten her.

They separated for a moment, but he didn't let go. When she opened her eyes, he hoped he wasn't imagining things and that there was in fact a glimmer of want in her gaze. He didn't have to wonder long as she clutched the front of his shirt and pulled him to her. This time when their lips met there was no hesitation. She kissed him with a longing he hadn't felt in a very long time, and as their kiss deepened, she moaned softly into his mouth and gripped him tighter. When they managed to let go, they were both breathless.

"Does this mean you'll give us a chance?" he asked.

She didn't answer him right away, which worried him, but then he caught her smiling and his fears vanished. "It means I want to take this one day at a time. No rushing. If that's okay with you."

He nodded in agreement, and when she laid her head on his shoulder, he felt a renewed sense of hope that had been lost for many years. God was finally filling in the missing pieces of his life, and he looked forward to what He might have in store for him and Hope...and Ivy too.

Noah pulled her into his embrace and kissed her forehead.

"If you're by my side, that's all that matters to me," he replied.

And it was the truth. As long as they were together, everything seemed possible. Together they could face anything – and he was more than ready for the journey.

AMISH DAWN

AMANDA REESE

Chapter 1: Times Like This

Dawn Wittmer always thought of herself as a simple girl, and was a simple girl in the eyes of everyone, except her parents. Everything that Dawn did was wrong. How could it be that such a simple girl was never good at doing anything? Dawn knew that her parents were quite strict, but still, she wondered why she never earned their satisfaction. Her parents' disapproval came out in ways that she preferred not to consider, such as her poor self-esteem. Even when she was selling the family's produce in the market she found herself stressed and worried that she would do something wrong, give incorrect change, or lose customers by not providing the service and prices that the customers wanted.

Dawn knew so little about life; sometimes she wanted her world to be just at least a little bit bigger than the world that her parents imagined for her. Dawn would have loved to have permission to just be a little bit, well, "normal." Some of her other Amish friends had permission to go out of the house, have English friends, and even on a rare occasion have a beer or a glass of wine. She didn't want to leave the Amish community but recently the way her parents had been treating her like she was a 7-year-old again was making her go crazy and feel more anxious.

Dawn wasn't seven years old and she knew that very well. She was 18 years old and graduating school this year. She'd learned more from studying on her own than she gained from attending school in the one room schoolhouse that her parents insisted she attend. Dawn dreamed of attending university, of becoming a nurse, and helping those who were sick. She didn't agree with everything that the Amish believed, such as their views regarding medicine and the use of it. Why shouldn't those who are very sick utilize medicine if they have the chance to make use of modern medicine that could save their lives? Why did her parents have to see everything in "black and white?" Everything was always good or bad. In other words, everything was Amish or English and if it was English that meant it was not acceptable.

If her parents knew about her views on medicine or that sometimes she drank wine with her friends they would be so angry that she probably could not stay in their home. What was so terrible about having a glass of wine? She wanted to know. The smell of a nice glass of Merlot or Cabernet Sauvignon would make her evening. Just that little feeling that lifted her mood ever so slightly. She could feel the stress melt away from her heart, her head, her soul, her body with just one glass of wine. Sometime when she visited her friend Beth Troyer they would sit and play Scrabble together, passing the time, laughing, and talking. What neither her parents nor Beth's parents knew was that an English friend of Beth's would buy her wine. Sometimes she paid her friend with money if she had any, and other times with baked goods.

Beth understood Dawn. They had been friends since they were little and even though neither one wanted to consider leaving the Amish community they had some complaints with the rules. Why were there so many rules?

Chapter 2: Market Days

Dawn's life continued. Her days at the market were long. Secret Scrabble and wine nights were few and far between. Plus, it was hard for Beth to sneak the wine into her room and get it cold. There was almost no way to get the wine cold unless her English friend brought the wine already chilled and they consume it immediately.

Among the rows of sellers in the market were both English and Amish vendors. The cost of renting the space was increasing yet their sales remained more or less the same. The same customers. The weeks melted into each other, seeming almost entirely the same. She hardly had any schoolwork to do and she knew that her parents would never let her attend college. What was the point? Recently one of the other storefront owners was coming around to her store almost every day. It was almost annoying. Actually, it was annoying. Sunny Landsdale was his name. He was a fairly tall young man with wide shoulders, and his hair was pulled back in a ponytail, as if he wanted to be a girl. His name sounded much like a name for a girl too. She thought he was a little strange, but perhaps some part of him could be likeable. Dawn's thoughts drifted to her Amish upbringing. God asks us to love everyone, not just the people we like or love. Certainly, it was her job to treat everyone with respect that came to her stand, whether or not she liked her family's customers. She convinced herself to make small talk with Sunny. She even wanted to get up the nerve to ask him why he didn't cut his hair. Maybe today would be the day she would ask him.

Among the other fruit and pastry sellers, Dawn sat at her stand amid crates of tomatoes, cucumbers, onions, garlic, corn, and even carrots when Sunny approached the stand again. Perhaps more annoying than his hair was the fact that he stopped by more or less just to chat. He didn't seem to have any objective except bothering her! Was this the goal? This could hardly be the goal. Of course, it also seemed strange that he would come and buy just a single tomato or onion. He claimed that he bought fresh ingredients every day to cook dinner. Dawn presumed that although this could be true, he also apparently came around to her stand just to speak to her. Although many other people would consider this a compliment she preferred to do her work and be left alone. Not to mention that she had heard some interesting things about him. Some stories that she hoped were not true. She heard he had multiple lovers, all customers. She didn't want to hear anymore.

"My dearest Dawn, you are looking beautiful as always. Although I bet you would look stunning in a long, sleek, black evening gown! You are quite a beauty. What can I say?" said Sunny. "Well, you could say less. That would be a great start," replied Dawn. "Oh, my lovely, one day you will be my wife, just you see! But, in the meantime I will have to wait for you to choose to leave your Amish community and run away with me. Of course, a man cannot wait forever!" declared Sunny with enthusiasm. Dawn rolled her eyes and asked him, "So, what can I get for you today, Mr. Landsdale: a single tom..." Sunny interrupted her midsentence. "I thought we discussed that my name is Sunny. Still you prefer to refer to me as Mr. Landsdale. Mr. Landsdale is my father, thank you very much."

"As you wish, Sunny," Dawn heard herself say. She couldn't help but thinking about how silly his name and hair were. Sunny laughed and Dawn paused before posing her question. "Mr. Landsdale, ahem, I mean, Sunny, did you ever realize that, between your hair and your name, some people may think some strange things about you. I don't mean to be rude, but you can hear all kinds of gossip about a boy with a name like Sunny!" Dawn offered this observation with some courage. Sunny simply laughed, "Actually, I love my name, and yes, my hair too. You wanted to ask about my hair, I'm sure. No?" asked Sunny. "Well, yes, I hadn't quite gotten there yet," said Dawn.

"Well, to tell you the truth, since you know, I'm always honest about everything, like your good looks for example... anyway, as I was saying. My Dad always cut my hair very short when I was a kid and I hated it. When I finally got old enough to make my own decisions about my hair, I decided to stop cutting it. My whole family went crazy, but then they got used to it, and I realized I actually quite liked it. So, I kept it. Now the hair goes better with my name too! It keeps people on their toes," answered Sunny.

"You certainly are at least an interesting person," answered Dawn. Sunny smiled as a slightly extended pause in the conversation ensued. "Right, anyway, I need three green peppers for dinner tonight," said Sunny. "Sure, wow. Three, not one?" joked Dawn. "Yes, three," echoed Sunny as a goofy grin spread across his face. Sunny handed over $1.00, took his green peppers and walked away back toward his stand.

Dawn found herself watching him as he walked away and couldn't understand what or why she was watching. He was such a strange man. Dawn shook her head and continued scouring the market, hoping to make eye contact with potential customers. Business had been slower than usual this summer with no thanks to the opening of a super Wal-Mart on the south side of the city. That's what she guessed anyway. It's difficult to maintain customers and gain new ones when giant corporations can roll into town and capitalize on the local people's inability to lower prices to an unreasonable point. As Dawn grew lost in her thoughts about the super Wal-Mart and even surprisingly about herself the market day grew to a close. She carefully put away all the unsold food, locked the cabinets, and made her way home by foot.

Chapter 3: A Patient Man

Jane and Mason Wittmer, Dawn's parents, did not see positive changes in Dawn. In fact, they were ready to sit down with their daughter and discuss with her their knowledge of this Sunny boy. Jane and Mason were respected by the entire Amish community and were well-known and respected even in the marketplace. It had come to their attention that Sunny Landsdale, a known associate of the Amish Mafia was purchasing goods from their store, which in and of itself, is not a crime. They did not appreciate, however, that he was making conversation with their daughter. Parents know best, of course. Anyone even vaguely connected with Amish Mafia was not a friend of theirs.

They didn't like what they know about Sunny. They even considered removing Dawn from the market stand to keep Sunny away from her.

Jane and Mason decided that they needed to sit down with their daughter and discuss this situation that was ever so pressing on their minds. A good Amish daughter did her work, stayed away from unnecessary conversation with any English man, worked on the farm or in the market, prayed, and did her homework. Dawn could be quickly headed down the wrong path. On the evening following the day of the three green peppers, Jane and Mason decided to summon their daughter to the sitting area.

"Dawn!" Jane called up the stairs. "We need you to come downstairs for a minute." Dawn immediately knew that those words meant "we want to have a serious conversation with you." A million and one things were passing through Dawn's mind. Did they found out that she and Beth had been sneaking wine into the community and drinking sometimes? Will they forbid her to apply to college?

"Dawn. We want you to stay away from the Sunny boy," said Jane. "Any questions?" asked Mason, Dawn's father. Dawn stayed silent. "No comment at all?" inquired her mother. "Well, yes: you know it's not my fault who comes to buy food at our store. What, you want me to put out a sign that says only GOOD people buy food here! Are you crazy?" said Dawn. "Enough!" shouted Mason. "We just want you to be a little careful with Sunny. Don't make conversation. Give him what he purchases and be sure to count the change extra carefully. Okay?" said Jane.

"Sure, Mom... whatever," answered Dawn as she rolled her eyes without realizing what she was doing until it was too late. "Not whatever, do not talk to your Mom with that tone of voice, and don't let me see you roll your eyes again!" shouted Mason. "Yes, Dad. May I be excused?" "Yes, thank you Dawn," whispered Jane in a small voice.

As Dawn crept back up the winding wooden staircase to her room she considered the conversation. Although she was annoyed by the way they had accused her of engaging in conversation with Sunny, she was more relieved that they didn't know about the wine. She wasn't a drunk. She didn't need a drink. She just liked a glass of wine once in a while. That hardly made her a sinner, or evil, did it? She didn't think that made her a sinner. In the Bible, Mary asked Jesus to turn water into wine during a wedding when the couple ran out of wine to serve their guests. Dawn silently recounted the parable to herself and reminded herself that she was not a bad person. She simply had difficult, traditional Amish parents.

She continued working at the market after the confrontation with her parents. But as if he'd been warned away, Sunny was suddenly making himself scarce. She wondered where he had gone. Was he okay? She chided herself for thinking about whether or not he was okay. Why was she worried about Sunny? Sunny, his girlish name, his bleached pony tail, and cocky smile. What a silly man; no... what a silly boy. How old was he anyway? After a week of managing the store in the market and seeing no sign of Sunny, Dawn was just about ready to accept that he had found another girl to flirt with. Or, perhaps, he'd left town. Types like Sunny didn't usually stick around too long. But just then there was a tap on her shoulder. "Good afternoon, Ms. Wittmer. How are you today?" asked Sunny. "Just fine, thank you, but um... where have you been?" asked Dawn.

"Ah! So, you missed me, right? I knew it! I knew you'd miss me!" replied Sunny, a huge grin spreading across his face. "No, I didn't say that. I just said, where have you been?" retorted Dawn. "Of course, as you see it. Busy. That's all," replied Sunny. "Okay, so what can I get you today?" asked Dawn.

"Well, actually, I don't need any green peppers, but I did want to know if you'd like to accompany me for a smoothie!" invited Sunny in a bright, ironically sunny way. "You mean, um, like a date?" asked Dawn. "Yes. Or no. Whatever you would like it to be," replied Sunny. "You know, I'm not... um, I'll think about it," said Dawn. "You'll think about it. Okay: well, I can be a patient man. Let me know, let's say tomorrow, about our non-date. It's just a smoothie," Sunny pointed out diplomatically.

With that, Sunny turned and walked backed into the crowd of the market. Dawn found herself standing at the counter trying to catch her breath. Yes, for certain, Sunny had just asked her out on a date. Were her parents correct in saying to stay away from him? What if they were just wrong about him? It wouldn't be the first thing they were wrong about. She never had English friends before because her family forbid it. She was just curious enough what it would be like to go out with an English boy that she contemplated saying yes. As she closed the store for the day she found herself poised between her family's values and wanting to discover herself and the world for herself.

Chapter 4: More Than Just Coffee

The next day as Sunny approached the counter, without even thinking Dawn said, "Yes." Surprised, Sunny said, "Ok then, I'll be back at close to 4pm to meet you!" As Sunny turned to walk away, Dawn said, "Wait, make it 3pm outside the back entrance of the market." "Anything for my sunshine!" replied Sunny and laughed, since, after all, his name was sunshine, not hers. At precisely 3pm Dawn closed the store one hour earlier than usual and met him outside the market. Dawn found Sunny waiting for her there. "It's just a few blocks away," said Sunny.

As they walked Dawn realized she didn't know what to say at all. It was as if someone had glued her lips together. Sunny, recognizing the pause and potential awkwardness, started talking about himself. "Well, since you don't know a lot about me, I'll tell you the saga, if you want." "Sure," answered Dawn.

"I grew up in several different foster homes, bounced from one to another, and usually I ran away because my foster parents would beat or just use me for the government check. You know?" Sunny began his remarkable tale as if it were commonplace. "Actually, I'm sorry, I'm not understanding, because you know I'm Amish," admitted Dawn. Sunny started again, in an attempt to clarify: "When I was young, my parents died in a car accident. I was 4 years old. Just old enough to remember them and miss them. When you become an orphan, or your parents don't want you, the state tries to find a placement for you with another family in another home. But sometimes, these homes are dangerous. There aren't enough controls and regulations on who can become a foster parent." "Oh, I'm sorry. I had no idea," said Dawn. "Don't be. I'm just sharing with you my story. As soon as I turned 18 I was out of the system because I became a legal adult. I was homeless for a little while until I found a job at one of the stands here. They pay me cash under the table. No taxes or anything. Since then I've saved enough money to get a place, but I've never finished school. I want to get my GED someday, but that seems like a dream." said Sunny.

There was another pause in the conversation, but this time, perhaps it was a needed pause. "And now, how are you?" Dawn asked with genuine concern. "I'm well, just me," said Sunny. "But, why did you tell me this other story about your hair and your parents, when you don't have parents?" asked Dawn. "I wanted to impress you," Sunny confessed. "I didn't want you think I was just some orphan kid. In the beginning, I kept my hair long because my foster parents would rarely give me a haircut, let alone pay for me to get one. Sometimes they would destroy my hair when they cut it. So, finally, when I aged out of foster care, I decided nobody was going to cut my hair like that again, even me," explained Sunny.

"Well, anyway, that's me. How about those smoothies?" Sunny invited, apparently ready to change the subject. "Of course," said Dawn. As they sat together in the Tropical Smoothie Café, Dawn imagined that in some ways she had never considered before, she'd been given more opportunities in her strictly controlled life than an English man like Sunny. She wanted to tell him that her parents would freak out if they knew she had come out with him even for a smoothie, but then again, she thought it might be better if she said nothing. He probably could have guessed as much anyway. As they continued talking, Sunny moved his hand across the table and placed it on top of Dawn's hand. Dawn was startled and considered moving it. But she found that she didn't want to move it. Nobody in the Amish community would be this open with another. No one would tell someone else who wasn't in his or her family personal things. Why couldn't she trust Sunny? It was true he was two years older than she was, but two years was nothing. Plus, they were both legal adults, and hand-holding wasn't a crime.

Finally, Dawn got up the nerve to ask Sunny about the gossip at the market. "Sunny, can I ask you something?" Dawn inquired. "Sure," replied Sunny. "Is it true that you... you know... with other girls. Like am I just one of a bunch of other girls?" asked Dawn. "Oh, no... actually I just ignore the gossip at the market. One of my old foster parents owns a stall in the market so they made up stories about me to try to make me lose my job, but it didn't work," replied Sunny. "Oh, I thought... sorry," whispered Dawn. "Don't be, it's not a problem."

Just then Dawn looked at the clock on the wall and realized it was 4:20. If she didn't all but run home her parents would know something was up. Dawn jumped up and said a little louder than necessary, "Oh, I have to leave quickly... if I don't get home soon..." "It's a problem, right? Your parents I'm sure wouldn't like seeing someone like me with their daughter. Right?" interrupted Sunny. "Actually, yes I'm really sorry. Please. I have to go. I'll see you tomorrow at the market?" asked Dawn, "Yes, don't worry, just g,." replied Sunny.

Chapter 5: Learning to Fly

They knew. Before Dawn even made it inside the door, Jane and Mason were waiting for Dawn at the kitchen table. How could I be so stupid, thought Dawn. Of course, someone would have noticed that she closed the store an hour earlier. As Dawn approached her parents, her father started screaming, so loud, that even the neighbors on the opposite end of the community would hear him. She was positive.

"Dawn. You're going to your uncle's! We're sending your disobedient soul away! You need to learn respect, and the importance of NOT LYING TO YOUR FAMILY! End of discussion! You will not go back to the marketplace tomorrow. You will not see Sunny Landsdale ever again! Do you hear me?" raged Dawn's father Mason.

Dawn stood in silence in the kitchen and held back tears. Mason continued screaming. "Do you know what filth people like Sunny are? He is nothing. Nobody. He is a cheater and he hangs around with the type of people we do NOT associate with! Do you understand me? We know for a fact that he has purchased a gun from the Amish Mafia. We don't know why he has a gun or wanted a gun, but you cannot speak to him ever again. ARE WE CLEAR?" bellowed Mason

Dawn could do nothing except nod her head yes. Then she ran to her room. She wanted to find Beth and tell her everything. She wanted even more to speak to Sunny. Her parents didn't understand him. They didn't know him. And if he owns a gun, Dawn was sure that there was a reason. Sunny was a good man. They didn't know anything. Who were her parents to tell her about Sunny anyway? Dawn was overcome with outrage. They knew nothing. How could it be that her parents never saw anything in another way? They saw only things the way they wanted to see them! Nothing else!

Tomorrow she would be sent away. The worst thing was that Sunny would once again have one less person to speak to. He was on his own. But what was worse? Having no family, or a family that doesn't understand you and let you be who you want to be? Family should be the center or everything, the center of life, the center of love. Without family we are alone—unless of course you believe in God. Even with God on your side, you can feel lost and alone. There is something unique about having a human companion. Dawn longed to have her own family and her own companion. For the last year or two, she had felt part of a family that, although she knew loved they her very much, she felt the need to be separated from them. Was it selfish, she wondered? Maybe it was just a part of growing up, she thought.

Dawn found herself lost in her own thoughts about life. As we grow up we see life in a different light, sometimes for better, and sometimes for worse. We learned to see things through our own lenses. We saw things the way we wanted to see them. Sometimes that was a better choice and sometimes not. We learned that life does not happen in black and white. Life is an ever-changing revolving door. As we grow up we learn that a whole world exists outside the bubble that our parents gave us. Then the only option we have is to make our decisions and choose whether or not we want to fly.

Chapter 6: Nowhere to Run or Hide

The events that followed the day of the smoothie were a blur to both Dawn and Sunny. Sunny went to Dawn's family's stand to find it closed. He was concerned but decided not to worry too much. For certain something had come up at home. Then again, that was also what he was worried about. What happened at home? Was it because he met her outside the market? Did someone see them together?

Sunny began panicking, but not too much, because like always, he found a solution. He knew how to handle almost every possible problem. Running he was good at. Actually, it was his specialty. So was hiding. The thing about being a former foster kid is that you learn how to run and hide. He didn't want to run this time. He finally had a job, an address, a roof over his head. Sunny passed the whole week trying not to be concerned when the stand didn't open. Finally, a week later the stand opened again, but still Dawn was nowhere to be found. A woman, probably Dawn's mother, was operating their fruit and vegetable stand. He knew that asking her where Dawn was could make things worse for Dawn so he simply passed the stand slowly looking for any sign that Dawn had been there or was okay.

As he passed the woman at the stand studied him with a fierce gaze. Her eyes followed Sunny across the market and watched his every move. Very conscious of the fact that he was being watched, he ducked out of the market and cut down an alley in the opposite direction of his apartment. If this was life, he wasn't sure why he existed. Perhaps worse than being orphaned was the knowledge that his mother had been pregnant when his parents died in the car crash. He never knew what it was like to have a sister or brother, but guessed that if he had been left with a brother or sister, at least they could have been there for each other.

Meanwhile Dawn woke up on the far side of the Pennsylvania border. The sun rose over Tennessee on her Uncle Kemp's property. Uncle Kemp was a quiet stern man with rules, a wood-burning stove, and a dog. Uncle Kemp never married and most of the family thought he was slightly strange. Dawn's uncle left the Amish years ago and was rarely in contact with his family. He left the community not because he minded the simple life, but actually, because he'd had a relationship with an English girl and was banished from the house. After the relationship ended, he didn't want to be with anyone else, quite literally. He took the failed union as a sign that he was to live alone.

Nobody even knew what he did to make a living and nobody asked either. Dawn found some small comfort in her Uncle's cooking and the dog, a Yorkshire Collie with thick white and black fur. She loved nothing more than to cuddle up to him, especially when she needed to cry, which was more often than not these days. She helped her Uncle Kemp in all but silence as she learned to cut wood for the fire, maintain the property, and prepare meals for the two of them.

Her parents must have thought that sending her away to her Uncle's would make her beg to come home. Dawn was not going to beg to come home. That was not part of her plan. She would stay here as long as they made her stay. She didn't care about anything. Well, almost anything. There was the issue of Sunny. She found herself thinking about where Sunny was or if Sunny thought she left the market to avoid him, or perhaps he thought that she didn't like him. Actually, the opposite was true. She was realizing that she did like him, more than she thought she did.

Chapter 7: Connections

The difficult part of finding a missing person is that either the person does not want to be found, or is being held against their will. There were few to no clues about the whereabouts of Dawn. Due to Sunny's long history of learning how to survive, hide, and get needed information, Sunny knew that if he was patient, eventually he would find out where Dawn had disappeared to. He lurked around the market listening for any information about her whereabouts. Most of the sellers at Amish community stands were tight lipped. If they knew something, they weren't telling. Many of the regulars didn't know anything about Dawn, but sellers at neighboring stands, with whom Dawn was friendly, surely did. About two weeks had passed before Sunny had a stroke of luck. He was standing in the line of shops behind the row where Dawn's family's store was located. He overhead a conversation that he had been waiting to hear.

"...too bad about Dawn, really. She is a nice girl," said the one candle shop owner.

"I always thought those Amish people were a bit strange," replied the lady who owned the pastry stand.

"You know, I heard they took her away entirely. To Tennessee, I think. Yeah, the mother said to me that she was going to her Uncle Kemp's place to stay awhile. Who knows how long she'll be gone," answered the candle shop owner.

"If I didn't know any better, I would have thought those two were together anyway. Maybe they were an item, you know," said the pastry stand owner.

"Anyway, it's better to keep your eyes to your own business," stated the candle shop owner.

That was all Sunny needed to hear. They took her out of state to Tennessee to an Uncle Kemp's house. Not as much information as he would have liked, but it was certainly a good start. It had been two weeks already since he last saw Dawn and he wasn't going to let the smoothie date be the last one.

Sunny informed his employer he was going on a personal business trip and hoped that he would still have his job and his apartment when he returned. He just paid the rent again so for now he would be okay.

Sunny left the next morning before dawn broke. He paused thinking about how lovely dawn was and how perfectly named his friend Dawn was. He would find her. With a one-way bus ticket to

Nashville, Tennessee, a granola bar, a water bottle, a change of clothes, an extra pair of boxers, a smartphone and charger, a half-full small notebook with a pen in the spiral binding, and a paper map of Tennessee in his backpack, Sunny boarded the Greyhound. Sunny knew Greyhound buses very well. More than once he'd had to utilize a fake ID to buy a Greyhound ticket to escape a foster family. Although Sunny mused it was probably unnecessary to find Dawn as she wasn't in any real peril, he felt somewhat obligated in that it was very likely his fault they took her away.

More importantly, he'd never felt like he could actually be with anyone before, the way he felt about Dawn. Despite all his jokes and flirting, he did truly have feelings for her. The bus to Nashville took a good sixteen hours. It could have been done in a lot less time, but the bus stopped in every little town known to man. How was it possible? Every hour that passed Sunny found himself getting more anxious, a feeling which was new to him. He was used to feeling in control, even when he was completely alone.

Upon arriving in Nashville, he appreciated the reality that Dawn could still be anywhere within the state. He only had the name "Uncle Kemp" to go on. Sunny found a café with a free Wi-Fi sign, ordered a grilled ham and cheese sandwich and a coke and politely asked for the password. The waitress gave him the password and quickly walked away. For certain he smelled like Greyhound bus. That was never a good smell. He always met the strangest people with unique stories on Greyhound buses, but this time, he wasn't interested in chatting with anyone.

A few minutes later, Sunny's grilled ham and cheese arrived with his coke, a pile of Lay's potato chips, and a dill pickle. After immediately devouring the sandwich, chips, and pickles, he opened his smartphone and typed in cities in Tennessee. He made a list of the largest cities of Tennessee and did a person search for the name "Kemp." There were only 13 Kemps listed in Tennessee and one of them must be the uncle.

One by one he found phone number for 11 of the 13 Kemps. He hoped that Dawn's Uncle Kemp was not one of the 2 Kemps that didn't have a phone number.

One by one he crossed off Kemps from the list. One number belonged to a woodworking business, another to a dentist's office, another three were disconnected, and a sixth and seventh number appeared to be retirees. Sunny was feeling all but completely discouraged as he made it to the 11th number. When he dialed it, a man answered the phone and said, "Hello, Kemp here." Sunny hung up immediately. The area code proved to be in Gatlinburg. Gatlinburg it was, then. Sunny rented a room for the night, got some rest, and started off early the next morning for Gatlinburg. Another Greyhound and then a few local buses later, Sunny stepped off into Gatlinburg.

Chapter 8: Fate

While Sunny was searching the town for Dawn's uncle, Dawn herself was in despair. When would she see Sunny again? Could she return to the market? What about her dream of becoming a nurse? Was her family ever going to come back for her? Reality started to sink in that maybe her mother and father were not coming back for her. She was trapped in Gatlinburg, Tennessee. As Dawn began to panic, Sunny grew closer to finding her.

As fate would have it, finally in a local McDonald's a cashier knew the name Kemp and told him where the man lived. The worker told Sunny "Yeah, he's just a few miles away. I live in that direction and I can drop you off on the right road when my shift is over." "Thanks, that would be great. Name's Sunny, by the way," said Sunny. Two hours later Sunny was sitting in a stranger's car and growing closer to his destination.

Dawn was outside in the woods preparing a fire for the evening as the sun began to set. Her Uncle was inside, quiet as usual, preparing some sausages for the fire, when Sunny rounded the bend in the road. Dawn was startled as she recognized him, screamed, and jumped up.

Her Uncle came running, and found an equal surprise in recognizing what was transpiring. Sunny, the boy that his sister wanted to keep away from his niece, has somehow tracked her down to this unlikely location. Well, since the boy was here already, there was no sense in throwing him back into the street at night. They would of course have separate rooms on opposite sides of the house.

The three found themselves face to face in front of the fire. Uncle Kemp approached Sunny before Dawn did. "So, you must be Sunny," said Uncle Kemp. "Yessir," replied Sunny. Uncle Kemp started slowly "Well, as you can see, I'm not too keen on visitors, but since you're already here, you may as well have a sausage or two."

Dawn carefully and awkwardly wandered over to Sunny as they embraced fully—not to mention quickly, as not to upset their host and make him uncomfortable. "I assume you two understand I take no responsibility for Sunny being here. And he will not sleep in the same room as you. Meanwhile, I should notify your parents that he's here, but I don't think that will be necessary," stated Uncle Kemp.

Uncle Kemp bowed his head and went inside to give them a few moments of privacy. "How did you find me?" asked Dawn. "I'm an ex-foster kid, remember. I know how to find anyone and how to lose anyone," replied Sunny. "Right, of course," said Dawn. "Look, I don't know what to say. I like you a lot. And I don't know how I feel about being stuck here in Tennessee," continued Dawn. Sunny replied, "Well, it sounds like a pretty awful thing, but your folks do care about you, I'm sure. They just care about you in a way that doesn't make sense for you."

Dawn leaned her head on Sunny's shoulder. His body was warm, his voice was endearing, but he very much needed a shower. "Um, Sunny, let's talk after you bathe. What do you think?" asked Dawn. "Haha, of course," replied Sunny. He chuckled as Dawn asked her Uncle if Sunny could shower. While Sunny cleaned himself, Uncle

Kemp left a clean pair of jeans and a plaid button-down shirt on the sink for him to wear.

To Uncle Kemp, Sunny seemed all right. Dawn and Sunny reminded him of when he was a kid. Kids want to be able to experiment in relationships. It's hard in today's world to keep an Amish kid within the confines of being Amish. After Sunny rejoined the fire the three sat together, lost in their thoughts. What they would do? Sunny and Dawn may care for each other a lot, but they had quite the decision to make, and soon. Uncle Kemp reluctantly told them his story about how he ended up living on his own. He told them about the English girl he fell in love with when he was 18. He told them it was their decision to make.

The fire dimmed and no logs were added to the dying embers. The night was not their friend, explained Uncle Kemp. He didn't believe in staying outside without the fire. The night belongs to evil. "We go inside," he said. Uncle Kemp showed Sunny where he could sleep.

Chapter 9: Dawn

Dawn arrived in a peculiar way. The sun rose quietly, the sky lit up with yellows, blue and even a little bit of orange. When the morning came, it seemed like there was no easy decision to make. There wasn't. Dawn could try to reconnect with her family, or she could stay and start over with Sunny. It was evident that Uncle Kemp was not going to stop them from making their own decision.

"Good morning, Dawn!" chanted Sunny. Sunny started singing and dancing circles around Dawn. As she laughed he pulled her into his arms and kissed her lightly on the lips. "Would you like to come with me? We can go anywhere we want," said Sunny with great optimism.

"I don't know, Sunny. We hardly know each other. You're a good boy, a good man, but I think we both have decisions to make." Dawn was trying to be even-handed and rational. Sunny tried to meet her halfway. "Let's do this, then. Let's go home. Ask your parents' permission to date me. We'll tell them everything. If they accept, that's great. If they don't, you have to decide what life you want for yourself, Dawn. Don't let them hold you back from anything. Be who you are," implored Sunny.

By 10am the two were packed and ready to leave with Uncle Kemp's blessing. He dropped them both at the highway with their backpacks and wished them the best. Since he was a man of few words, his last sentence was only one: "Godspeed."

Dawn and Sunny both nodded and found their way back to the center of Galinburg. Soon they were at the Greyhound station once more. A few hot dogs from a food truck proved to be enough to fill their stomachs as they made their way to Nashville. In Nashville, they decided to press forward through the night on an overnight bus. The whole way Dawn and Sunny found themselves engaged in pleasant conversation. Sunny admitted that he had a gun, but it was only to defend himself. Dawn needed no more explanations, only peace, time, and patience. She fell asleep in his arms on the bus as it rolled along through the night.

They washed themselves at Sunny's house in the morning and planned to go to her parents' house the next morning at dawn, for which she was well named. Dawn knocked on the door with Sunny next to her side. The door opened and she said, "Hi Mom. This is Sunny. He is my boyfriend. If you can accept us both, we'd like to come inside."

AMISH ROSE

SABRINA VICKS

Chapter 1: Saying Goodbye

She pictured a flower, however, instead of it blooming towards the sun, it folded inward, protecting the center. She and her daughters were the center and it would stay that way for a year when people would come to her dwelling every Sunday to sit with the family in mourning. For a year they would adorn themselves in the appropriate black attire and show nothing on their faces, no feelings, no tears. At least for that last part she would not have to pretend.

For three days, she would tend to her duties knowing that his grave was getting deeper. The body was prepared as was the coffin—simply and cleanly, in accordance with tradition. People from all over the community came to the viewings—first at their home, then at the funeral, and finally, at the gravesite where his body was laid to rest. She did not struggle through the proceedings because unlike other funerals she had heard of where the family and friends gather around and tell stories of remembrance and honor of the deceased, all she had to do was muster enough energy to thank the Lord. Which she did with all of her heart because she was truly thankful.

Once the last of the visitors left her home, she felt as if for the first time in a long time her lungs could actually fill with air. A great deal of pressure had been released from her chest and she no longer felt as though the world were rolling on top of her—but it had nothing to do with mourning the loss of her husband and everything to do with finally being able to rejoice it with no eyes on her to witness the impropriety. She was no longer Rebecca the married, she was now Rebecca the widow.

"Mama," her youngest daughter, Sarah, called out to her from the door frame. She was dressed in her long white nightgown with her simple bonnet covering her long, raven black hair. Her mother often wondered where her daughter got her striking beauty and she often felt as though she may envy her a little too. Such a pure beauty—she could not be missed unlike her mother who was easily overlooked in a crowd. "Mama?" Sarah said quietly, taking a few steps toward her mother.

"Yes, Sarah. I'm awake, it's alright. Come sit by me," Sarah snuggled in close to her mother and rested her head in the small crook her mother made between her arm and stomach. "You should be asleep now."

"I know, mama. I just couldn't sleep," her eight-year-old daughter glanced up at her with her clear blue eyes and her mother saw them as two pools of untainted honesty.

"I could not sleep, either" Rebecca confessed. "What thoughts do you have in your mind that are disturbing your sleep?"

"Every time I close my eyes, I see the men lowering him into the grave and he reaches the bottom. But when I look into the grave to say goodbye, the coffin is open and he is not inside," Sarah looked into the distance as she recounted her nightmares, "I'm afraid."

"It is normal, Sarah, for a daughter to miss her father once he has left this earth. We just have to remind ourselves that this was the Lord's plan and while we may not always understand it, we must always have faith in it. We must always stay true to Him and thank Him for his blessings."

"I am not sad, mama," Sarah whispered quietly, "I'm afraid he will come back." Her mother looked down at her daughter knowingly and she sighed—not out of frustration or impatience—out of an indescribable silence that her daughter had to endure her first eight years in such a way that she would be afraid of her dead father.

"I understand, Sarah. He won't be coming back, I promise you that. Once he died, his soul left his body and a body cannot move or breathe on its own. It must have the soul in order to live," Rebecca paused. She felt too tired to get into a lecture on life and death so she added this, "This is why it is important for us to protect and preserve the integrity of our souls." Sarah nodded sleepily as she wiped at her eyes. "Go to sleep, Sarah. We have to start anew tomorrow and we must be at our best."

Sarah got up and walked down the short hallway to her room which she shared with her sister, Ruby. Rebecca heard Sarah climb into bed and mumble something quietly to herself.

Rebecca stayed where she was and recalled the last few months. She looked down at her arm and pulled up the sleeve of her dress to reveal the dark bruise just above her elbow. Fingers wrapped around her arm forcing her into her place. *It is ironic*, she thought, *the man who gave me this is gone but the bruises still remain.* She pulled down her sleeve again and looked out the window to the spot in the garden where she merited such a reaction.

"Rebecca!" Tom yelled from the top step of the house.

"Yes, Tom?" She wiped the sweat from her brow as she stood up from her garden bed. The sun was beating down with such force that she could feel each breath turn hot against her lips as soon as she exhaled. She watched as her husband came over to where she was standing and she could tell from the way he pulled his eyebrows together and twitched up the right side of his mouth that he was unhappy with something. "Girls," Rebecca said to her two daughters, "mind the rest of the rows, please. I need to go inside to talk with your father."

"Do you need help?" Ruby asked, peering over her shoulder at her father's expression.

"Young lady, did you hear what your mama told you to do?" her father spoke quietly, but he was the very definition of a calm before a storm.

"Yes, sir. Sorry, sir." Ruby and Sarah turned back to the garden and continued their work as their mother walked inside following their father.

"Would you like some water, Tom?" Rebecca asked her husband.

"No," he stared out into the garden and watched the two girls working. "Those girls are lazy and they are not fulfilling their duties as respectable women."

"Tom, they are eight and ten years old. They work hard every day helping me around the house to clean and make sure food is prepared when you come home. They have been in the garden with me all day despite how hot it is today."

"This is just like you," he scoffed, "you are always making excuses for them! How can you expect them to grow up when you are always there to coddle them?"

"I am not coddling them, I—" Tom directed his glare at Rebecca and she froze midsentence. This is it, she had somehow pushed him to this point again and he was not going to let her walk out of here without learning a lesson his way. He reached toward her and grabbed her by the arm, pressing down so hard that she could already feel her fingers tingling from lack of blood flow. "Tom, please. I understand. I will make them work harder. I promise you!"

"They have learned laziness from your example. If you ever desire our daughters to succeed, you need to fix yourself first." He released her arm and took another small step forward so that his nose rested softly against her own. "You reap what you sew, Rebecca. Never forget that."

His words lingered in her mind and Rebecca snapped open her eyes and slowly realized that she had fallen asleep thinking about the exhausting events over the past few days. She blew out the candle and to the night air she said, "Goodbye, Tom."

Chapter 2: The Healing

The girls woke up in the morning and came to the breakfast table where they began preparing their usual morning cereals and oatmeal. Rebecca woke a bit later than she was used to and she was surprised to find the girls working so efficiently with no supervision.

"Well, good morning girls. It seems as though you have all gotten a good night rest," Rebecca said pleasantly as she prepared her own breakfast meal.

"Didn't you sleep well, mama?" Ruby asked, "I know I did for the first time in a long time." Rebecca looked at her eldest child and although she shared the same black hair as her sister, Ruby was plainer than Sarah. She had small freckles which lined her nose and thin lips stretched across her face. But despite her looks, Ruby was a sharp young girl and she often sounded and acted more mature than any of the other girls her age.

"I slept well," Rebecca conceded and she caught a sideways glance from Sarah prior to continuing, "Today we will have to tend to the livestock and we will also have to start harvesting our crops."

"Mama, when we are finished working, can I go to play with Mary? She's invited me to go down by the river with her to read."

"You may, Ruby," Rebecca nodded at her daughter and then added, "Bring Sarah with you." Sarah looked at her mother and then at Ruby who just shrugged her shoulders and kept eating.

"Mama, are you sure you want to be alone?" Sarah finally asked.

"It will be okay, Sarah. We will focus on our tasks for the day and keep our minds prayerful and everything will be okay." Ruby looked between her mother and sister not fully understanding the conversation taking place, but she decided not to bother trying to examine it further than face value.

The days turned into months and their harvest was growing steadily. The hard work provided a welcome distraction for Rebecca and her girls as they all tried to move forward with their lives.

The day was much cooler than when they had planted the crops so the work did not seem as difficult. The women worked hard with few breaks in order to complete their tasks efficiently. Once it was time to check the livestock and feed them, Rebecca told the girls that they could go meet with Mary. She watched as the girls skipped happily with each other, hand in hand, towards the direction of the river.

Rebecca finished tending to her livestock and she went back into the house. It was still early in the morning and she had already finished a great deal of work. While she sat there, she couldn't help but feel a bit sad about losing Tom. He was not the most righteous man in the entire world, but he tried to have the best intentions. Rebecca recalled memories which were much sweeter when he began to court her, oh how he had made her smile. Now all of her memories are muddled together in a dark grey matter and she cannot decide what to feel anymore.

In that moment, with her girls gone to the river, Rebecca decided to go to a service away from her own community. She needed fresh faces and above all, she needed space. Space to talk with the Lord and be honest with herself and with Him about what she was feeling about her whole situation. She felt good, but the guilt that came with that was almost overwhelming and she needed the peace that only He could provide.

She went outside and hooked up the buggy. She drove it outside of her own small community, waving at the people who noticed her and keeping her eyes forward. It wasn't that far to the nearest community and she hoped that being away from it all would help her to gain some much-needed perspective.

As she pulled into the community, she leaned out of her buggy to a young woman walking past her carrying a pail of water. "Excuse me," she called out to the passerby. The young woman glanced at her and smiled.

"You're not from here, are you?" she asked Rebecca.

"No," Rebecca replied sheepishly, "I come from the community very near to here. I just wanted to—well, I was wondering if you could point me in the direction to the nearest service."

"I am headed there myself, feel free to follow me."

Rebecca offered to give the woman a ride to the house, and she climbed in beside Rebecca pointing the way to the house where the service was to be held that morning. The son of the house came out to greet the woman whose name Rebecca learned was Emma.

"I'm sorry," the boy apologized as his cheeks reddened from embarrassment, "I can't seem to remember your name."

"She's new here, Eli. You do not need to be ashamed!" Emma exclaimed with a friendly smile.

"Oh!" Eli said, clearly relieved. He offered to take her horse into the stable while the women went inside to talk amongst themselves before the service began.

Emma walked ahead of Rebecca and introduced her to all the women in the house. Finally, they came to Eli's mother, Naomi, who was hosting today's service. "Hello, Emma," the woman pulled her in for a quick hug, "and who do we have here?"

"Hello, my name is Rebecca. I come from the community near to here and I wanted to come for a service," she explained.

"We are all happy you could join us!" Naomi said, "Is your husband with the other men?"

Rebecca paused a moment before responding. She knew this was already a strange situation for a woman from another community to come all the way here for a service and she did not want to get into a conversation regarding her newly appointed status as a widow, so she replied, "I am not married."

"Ah," the woman said, looking at Rebecca up and down. She smiled but it did not reach her eyes and Rebecca knew that the other women in the group would start forming their own opinions about her now. She had just wanted to get away from the eyes that knew her sad story, but now she found herself amongst eyes that assumed her sad story, which felt even worse.

Rebecca walked over to a bench where Emma sat and the service soon began. The first preacher stood in front of the community and began speaking.

"Trust in the Lord with all your heart and lean not on your own understanding. These are the words that we read in Proverbs, but do we truly live by them?" he asked, "Can we consider ourselves righteous and people of faith if we only read words and do not act on them or incorporate them into our own daily lives? No, those of us who do not believe in the Lord's plan, we cannot claim to be righteous. Those of us who believe only in our own selves, our own hearts, our own minds—we forget that these do not belong to us alone. They belong to everyone, they belong to Him. We are all part of his plan and the Lord will giveth and taketh away as His will commands. Whether we understand—rather, whether we choose to try to understand, this is where we fail."

Rebecca glanced around the room at all the bobbing heads who were taking in the words with open minds and open hearts. She closed her eyes and reflected on her own situation and in the deepest corners of her heart, she felt relief. She decided in this moment, that she should not feel unhappy or guilty—the Lord's plan took Tom from her life for a reason. The Lord's plan gave her comfort and a chance at finding happiness again. Although she did not understand it, she would never fully understand it, she knew in this moment that she did not need to.

Chapter 3: The Meeting

The end of the service came around and the men and women separated to enjoy their meals and reflect on the words spoken.

Emma walked next to Rebecca as they found a place on the benches to sit and talk together. "How did you enjoy the service?" Emma asked.

"It was exactly what I needed to hear," Rebecca replied, smiling. "The Lord certainly does work in mysterious ways." Emma nodded in agreement. "Emma, I must share something with you about earlier."

"What is it?" Emma asked her new friend.

"When I was speaking with the woman earlier, I told her that I was not married. While that is technically true, it is not the whole truth," Emma pulled her eyebrows together as a puzzled look came across her face. Rebecca continued, "I was married. My husband, he—well, he passed away a few months ago. I have two beautiful young daughters that I cherish with all of my heart, but I needed to go to a place on my own to listen to my heart and hear what the Lord needed me to hear."

"Oh my," Emma said, reaching for Rebecca's hand, "well as the sermon said today, the Lord giveth and taketh away as His will commands. So, we should thank Him for his undying presence in our lives making all things possible for us through Him."

Rebecca smiled kindly at her new friend, sincerely feeling happy that she had the chance to meet Emma. The two women finished their meal and offered to help hand out the coffee and iced water to all the members. As she walked around offering the beverages among the men, she caught the eye of one man sitting on a bench talking with the son that Rebecca had met earlier.

"Rebecca!" Eli called out to her. She walked over to where he was sitting and offered him a drink. "No, thank you. I have water already. Have you met Jacob yet?"

"No, I have not." Rebecca looked over at the man sitting on the bench and she could feel her face growing warmer as she took in his tanned face and his respectfully groomed deep brown beard. But what struck here even more were his green eyes—they reminded her of spring and grass and fresh, healthy crops, and the innocence of childhood when everything seemed possible.

The man coughed quietly bringing Rebecca back to the present. "I said it is nice to meet you. Where are you from?" He smiled at her tenderly causing her face to turn red once more.

Eli answered for her, "She is from a community near to here. Emma knows her!"

"Ah," the man responded, "Emma is my youngest sister."

Rebecca finally unfroze and managed to say, "Yes." He looked at her quizzically and then she quickly added, "I mean yes, I am from a community near to here. And yes, I met Emma today. She is a beautiful woman who has helped me in many ways already."

"Yes, she has a keen ability of getting along well with everyone." Rebecca smiled at the man and then he added, "Well, I don't want to keep you from your duties much longer. It was nice meeting you."

"Right, of course. Thank you!" Rebecca walked away from their bench and headed back inside to the kitchen where she placed the pitchers. She found Emma in the kitchen already, waiting for her.

"Emma, I've just met your brother, Jacob. He was very kind."

Emma smiled warmly, "Yes, he is the best brother. He always helps me when I need it and it seems he cannot say no to me!" She laughed at her own private joke.

Rebecca looked down at her feet, for some reason the comment Emma made felt too intimate to share with someone that she had just met. She looked back up to find Emma toiling with the pitchers as she prepared a new coffee. "Well," Rebecca started, "I suppose I should get going. I do not want to leave my daughters for much longer. I imagine they may be hungry."

"Daughters?" A woman behind her gasped. Rebecca turned and found that it was the woman of the house, Naomi. "You are not married!" Rebecca saw other women turn to glance in their direction, not ashamed to show the disbelief on their faces.

"I apologize for misleading you, Naomi," Rebecca looked around the room suddenly feeling as if the walls were closing in on her. She was trying to explain herself, but the right words were failing her.

Emma stepped up next to her, "She is a widow," she offered, "She did not want to expose herself as he was just recently buried."

Naomi took a step back and placed her hand on her heart, "Oh, my dear. I am so sorry I assumed—I always chastise myself for doing that! I hope that you and your family find peace as this is all just a part of the Lord's plan."

"I know," Rebecca responded, finding her voice again, "We are doing well and trying to move forward with things." The women around her nodded in agreement and each one offered a supportive smile.

"We will pray for you," Naomi added before turning back to her friends.

"Well, as I said, I should be getting back now." Emma took Rebecca's hand and led her outside where they called to Eli.

"I must be going, Eli. I want to thank you for your generosity today, it is most appreciated." Eli smiled and then went into the barn to retrieve her horse. To Rebecca's surprise, it was Jacob who walked out with the horse instead.

"I believe this is yours," Jacob said, grinning.

"Yes," Rebecca reached for the straps, but Jacob held them a moment longer.

"You should come here again."

"Oh? Why is that?"

"I would like to invite you on a walk. I would have asked now, but I know that you have to leave," he explained, "I want to get to know you better." Rebecca was unsure how to respond to this, it appeared as if she met him for a reason and she knew that never before had a man inspired these feelings, not even Tom. *Especially not Tom,* she thought. But how would she explain herself to this man? What would the other women think as they all knew the truth about her situation?

She stopped for a moment and recalled the words from the sermon earlier in the day, *whether we understand—rather, whether we choose to try to understand, this is where we fail.* She did not understand what was happening or why, but she trusted that her response was the right one.

"I would love to."

Chapter 4: The Rendezvous

As she laid down that night, her mind was racing with thoughts of Jacob. She imagined them walking along the river and talking about everything. She knew that she would not be able to hide the truth from him about Tom and her daughters, but she did not want to. She wanted him to know her as she truly was, nothing more and nothing less. She did not know how he would respond, but again, she trusted that they had met for a reason.

She closed her eyes as she dared to imagine him holding her hand as they sat in the grass, staring out into the water. She drifted off to sleep with the sweet beginnings of a dream in her mind.

The next few days went by without anything remarkable and she was grateful for the routine of it all. They woke up and tended to their chores, the afternoons were typically filled with prayers and meeting with friends in the community. She didn't allow herself to think too much of the impending reunion with Jacob for fear that he would not accept her. *He could already know the truth*, Rebecca thought to herself, *all the women know. Emma knows, she may have said something to him.* She forced the thought to the back of her mind before she let it affect her anymore.

The day came and she was preparing the buggy when Sarah walked up to her, "Mama, where are you going?"

"I am going to the community down the way, Sarah," Rebecca looked at her daughter, "I told you and Ruby this last night over supper. Do you not remember?"

"Oh," she looked down at her feet and quietly admitted, "I had forgotten."

"It's alright, Sarah. Sometimes we forget things if we weren't really listening."

Sarah looked up at her mom and asked, "Can I go too, mama?"

"I thought you were playing with your sister?"

"They do not want to play with me today," she said with a disappointed look. Rebecca turned to face her daughter and for the first time in a while, she recognized just how young she truly was. She had her entire life ahead of her.

"Well," said Rebecca taking Sarah into a tight embrace, "I bet if you start playing a fun game, they will ask to play with *you* instead!" Sarah looked at her mother with a big smile and skipped off into the distance, no doubt to find Ruby and her other friends. Rebecca finished preparing the buggy and climbed aboard ready to face Jacob for the first time since the service.

The ride to the community felt longer than the last time and Rebecca hadn't even thought about what she would say to him when she saw him or how she would start the conversation. She quickly realized that she had no idea which house was his or where she might be able to tie up her buggy. Gripped with panic, she was tempted to turn around. *This is too soon*, she told herself, *I am not supposed to be here.*

Just as the thought came to her, she saw him standing there in the middle of the entrance to the community. She smiled to herself and slowed down in order to speak to him.

"Hello, Rebecca."

"Jacob," she nodded towards him trying to rid the smile from her lips and failing.

"You can follow me, I will show you where to park the buggy." She followed closely behind him and he led her to a small barn behind a house. The door to the house swung open and Emma came running outside.

"Rebecca!" she called out. The two women embraced as if they had been friends for years. They laughed together while Jacob took the horse to the stable. "Jacob told me that you would be coming back today. At first, I was confused because there is no service, but then I realized what he was talking about!" she quickly added, "But don't worry, I don't think anyone else knows but me. It's our little secret!" Emma let out a girlish giggle and for the first time, Rebecca realized that Emma must have been at least five or so years younger than herself. She smiled at the girl as Jacob walked towards them both.

"Do I even want to know what you two are talking about already?" Jacob asked playfully.

"Shh," Emma laughed, "He's here!" The two women laughed as Jacob shook his head, but the smile never left his face.

"I thought maybe we could talk a walk by the river," Jacob offered. Rebecca nodded and looked back at Emma who was waving from the stoop.

They walked quietly next to each other for a few minutes before Jacob said, "My sister is quite fond of you."

"Well, from what you have told me, she can be quite fond of everyone."

"This is true," he smiled. Rebecca took a moment to admire his smile—it wasn't perfect, his teeth were not lined up neatly in a row and they did not necessarily sparkle, but his smile was so genuine, it lit up his entire face, and it made the recipient want to smile as well.

"How old is she?" Rebecca asked, "If you don't mind my asking that question."

"Of course not. Emma is now seventeen years old. She is my youngest sister. I have another sister, Mary who is nineteen. I am above her at twenty-two. And then my eldest two sisters, Lorna and Lucinda, they are twins and they are twenty-five. Lorna and Lucinda are both married and live in this community as well."

"Wow, what a blessing to have such a large family. And to be the only boy, that must be fun!" Rebecca joked.

"I like to think I am the greatest body guard that ever lived," he laughed, "Except for the fact that nothing has ever happened to them, so it's been a pretty mundane job." He looked at Rebecca and asked, "So, how about you? Do you have any brothers or sisters?"

"No, I'm afraid. It is just me," Rebecca looked out towards the water as she thought about her life as a child and how lonely she had always been with no siblings to play with. She thought of her own daughter, Sarah, from today and decided that it would be now or never. "I do have two daughters, Sarah and Ruby."

"Yes, Emma told me about them," Jacob said. Rebecca stopped walking suddenly and Jacob turned to face her, "What is it?"

"She told you?"

"Yes, I asked her why you needed to leave from the service and she told me that you had to get home to your daughters."

"Did she tell you anything else?"

"No, that was all. Was that wrong of her to share that information? I'm sorry if that upset you in any way..." he trailed off.

"It isn't that," she sighed, "I just, I didn't know that you knew that and I didn't want to think poorly of me."

"Why would I think poorly of you?"

"My husband, Tom. He recently passed and now it is just the three of us. I did not want you to think—"

"Rebecca," Jacob cut her off mid-sentence and she looked up at him with tears in her eyes. *How foolish*, she thought, *I am crying before a man I hardly know.* "Rebecca, I do not want you to take this in the wrong way at all, but I deeply believe in the power of God's will and I know that He has a plan for all of us. What has happened in your life was just

Him making room for what is to come next. We cannot expect you to be grateful to Him for what He has done while also living in the past, unable to move on from it. Here," Jacob held out his hand to her, "take my hand and with every step we take, we move further away from what has happened and move closer to the rest of life's possibilities."

Rebecca looked at his outstretched hand and hesitated for a moment before finally deciding to place her hand in his. He smiled at her and they walked along the edge of the river talking about their families and their lives. Rebecca told him about Tom—both the happy and the not-so-happy times. They walked until the sun started to dip below the horizon.

"I should be going," Rebecca said to Jacob, finally releasing his hand. He nodded and walked her back to the barn where he went inside to retrieve the horse. Emma came running outside of the door as if she had been waiting for their return.

"You must stay for dinner!" she announced.

"I cannot today, Emma. I am sorry. I have to get back to my girls."

"Oh right, of course. Well the next time you come, you must bring them with you!"

"The next time?" Rebecca laughed.

"He did ask you to come back again, didn't he?" Emma looked around for her brother, "Jacob! You didn't ask her to come back again?" she said in utter disbelief.

Jacob laughed at his youngest sister, "I was getting there, Emma."

"Oh," Emma said and her cheeks flushed, "I'm just going to go back inside now." She gave Rebecca a quick hug and ran inside of the house.

"Would you like to come back soon?" He looked so hopeful and Rebecca thought back on the afternoon they spent together. She felt at peace and it was so easy to talk to him about everything.

"I was thinking," Rebecca said quietly, "perhaps you could come to my community. I'd like for you to meet my girls." Jacob beamed at her and nodded in agreement. He helped her onto her buggy and when

Rebecca looked back to give him a final wave goodbye, she saw that his eyes had never left her.

Chapter 5: The Meeting

The next day Rebecca and the girls spent the entire day cleaning the house from top to bottom, ensuring that everything was for Jacob's arrival. Rebecca's mother and father came in the afternoon while the girls were busy getting ready.

"I see you are having no trouble keeping things in order," her mother commented. "I don't think I have ever seen the house so clean."

"We are expecting a guest from a different community in a short while," Rebecca explained, slightly off put by her mother's comment.

"Who is coming?" her father asked.

Rebecca looked at the man who sat across from her and took in his sturdy frame built from years of arduous work. Little pieces of grey hair had just started speckling his beard and hair, the only indication of his age. She loved her father dearly and she knew that he wanted his only daughter to be happy.

"Jacob," she replied, "I met him at a service last week." Her mother glanced at her father and waited for his reaction.

"You've invited a man to your home? Rebecca, I do not like this at all," her father pulled at his beard as he always did when something made him uncomfortable.

"Father, I wanted him to meet the girls. And I thought it would be better for all of us if he could meet them where they are most comfortable, in their own home."

"Meet the girls?" her mother exclaimed, "Have you thought about what you are doing? What if others see a man walking into your home knowing that your husband is no longer here?"

"Mother, how can I move forward and truly accept God's plan if people expect me to constantly live in the past?" Her father nodded slowly and folded his hands on top of one another.

"We would like to meet him," he said finally. Neither Rebecca nor her mother thought it wise to go against him so they quietly gave in to him. The girls emerged from their rooms looking as beautiful as ever and ran into their grandparent's arms giving them tight hugs.

The five of them talked amongst themselves until they heard a small knock at the door. Her father stood up and walked over to the wooden entrance, pulling open the door. Jacob reached out his hand immediately and introduced himself. Rebecca's father invited him inside of the house and they all sat and talked about the girls and the communities. They talked about their faith and Rebecca could tell that both her mother and her father were impressed by the strength of Jacob's character.

He is a good man, Rebecca thought to herself, *perhaps I needed to know what life was like before him so that I could truly appreciate the goodness within him.*

Rebecca looked around the room admiring the feeling of warmth and love, a feeling that she had strived for a long time to achieve. Perhaps she didn't fully understand why things happened as they did, but she did know one thing. Whatever God's plan for her, Jacob was certainly a part of it.

GOING HOME

JENNIFER MCDONALD

Rebecca stared at the house. Her eyes didn't see the neat gardens or the paint that had obviously been applied recently, and which kept the house looking tidy. They didn't see the obvious work that the people within, her parents and siblings, had done on it to keep it nice.

All her eyes saw was the fire, the smoke, the broken remnants of the car that had taken her Eli from her.

When she'd talked to him about coming home, it had always been assumed that they would go together. That when they got here, it would be to announce their marriage, and that their families would have to just accept it. They had saved enough money to set up their own house, and that was what she had always assumed would happen.

Now here she was. Crawling back to her parents. Alone and scared and without Eli's comforting presence at her side. She was going to have to face her mother and father for the first time since she'd walked out two years ago.

The plan had been simple, back then. While Rebecca's parents had approved of the potential marriage between her and Eli, Eli's parents had not. They had a different girl in mind for him, and while it was his choice, the pressure they'd put on him to accept their choice had been overwhelming.

So why not leave? Go into the wider world, the one that both of them had only just barely glimpsed during their Rumspringa, and make it on their own? Have some fun, away from the restrictions that his parents, in particular, wanted to put on them?

They'd been eighteen then. It had been two years since then. They'd made the money, working two jobs each. Neither of them had ever been afraid of hard work.

When it came down to it, though, neither of them had ever been comfortable, really, with living together, with living in sin. When they'd both admitted to that, everything had seemingly fallen into place.

They would go home. They would get married before they did so that no one could tear them apart, and then they would raise their kids away from the big city. Philadelphia, they'd both agreed, was no place to raise children. It would be too expensive, and far, far too immoral.

Then came the night that Eli had come to pick her up from work. He'd always been a gentleman like that. He'd learned to drive while in the big city, though, and she hadn't, so even though he was exhausted from his own job, he'd gotten into his cheap, secondhand car and drove through the bad part of town to come get her.

Neither of them had seen the drunk driver coming. Rebecca had been thrown free. She'd walked away from the horrific accident with nothing more than a few bruises, but Eli ...

Blinking back tears, Rebecca straightened her shoulders and forced her eyes to come back into focus. She had to see what was in front of her. She was alone, and she would continue to be alone unless she could get her parents to agree to take her back.

Maybe she could have kept living in the city, but the rent there was so expensive, especially for one person. Besides, without Eli, it didn't feel quite right. Nothing did. Going back home was the only option that she had, and part of her, quite a large part, yearned for it.

Life had been exciting in Philadelphia, but it had also been complicated. Complex. Life with her parents had always been simple, and she craved that simplicity now just as much as she had rebelled against it two years ago.

She'd thrown away most of her Amish clothing when she'd left for the big city, but thankfully, she'd kept one dress and her white bonnet. When she looked down at herself, she looked much as she had on that fateful day when she and Eli, full of hopes and dreams, had walked away and hadn't looked back. Not until years later, anyway.

She just hoped that it wasn't too late.

Taking a deep, deep breath, she let it out slowly, forcing the tears from her eyes. Philadelphia didn't feel like home, but neither did her parents' house. Was there anywhere on the planet for her anymore? Or had she, with her recklessness, lost that forever?

How long she would have stood there, just staring, she didn't know. But she heard the familiar squeaks, the heavy clip-clop of horse's feet, and moved out of the way of the buggy that she knew was coming without having to give any thought to it at all.

As she moved, she looked to see who was driving the buggy. The man she saw there was no different from many of the other men in their settlement, at least on the surface. He was bearded, dressed all in black, a hat perched atop his head. It had been strange, in the big city, seeing people who didn't wear hats most of the time ...

And then her eyes met the man's, and she flinched away. Eli's brother, Samuel, looked back at her, just for a second, his eyes burning into hers. There could be no doubt that he recognized her.

The buggy rolled on, and Rebecca drew one deep, shuddering breath into her lungs, which had been starved of oxygen through the entire encounter. Samuel, who would doubtless go tell his father and mother, who had never much cared for Rebecca and surely now despised her, would soon know that she was back.

That thought provided her the impetus that she needed. It was enough to have her walking around the yard and up the stairs, her sensible black shoes muffled as she went to the door and knocked on it firmly.

It was her mother who answered the door. Her mother, who looked just the same as she always had, with her kind, dark eyes. Her mother, and until Rebecca laid eyes on her again, she hadn't realized just how much she actually missed this woman.

She hadn't meant to cry, she really hadn't. She'd been pushing tears back ever since the accident that had taken Eli away from her. Strange to think that it had only been a week ago. It felt like it had been a lifetime since he'd last touched her.

When her mother opened her arms to Rebecca without a word, that was all it took to rip down that wall that she'd put up around her heart. The wall that had let her do what it was necessary for her to do, which had held back all of her emotions and let her put her affairs in order so that she could make her way home.

Home. Home was in her mother's arms, crying on her shoulder. Home was the rest of the family, her three brothers, and her baby sister, coming out to greet her, to wrap her up in family affection that did a fair bit to salve the pain inside her.

Family was where, when you had to go there, they had to take you in. She'd heard it said as a joke, but in that moment, she knew that it was also nothing but the truth.

* * *

"Rebecca King, I need to speak with you," Miriam, her mother, said firmly. It was a week after Rebecca had come home, and she knew that she hadn't been very useful in that time. She had helped her mother around the house, with the cooking and the cleaning, a little bit, but that was it.

It was unlike her, and her mother, who knew her better than most people did, would know that.

Rebecca closed her eyes briefly, trying to brace herself for what was going to come next. Demands about what she'd done while she was in the city, perhaps. Questions about Eli, though Rebecca knew that their community had received news about Eli's death. She knew because she'd been the one to send it to his parents. They would have gotten the letter she'd sent the day after the accident.

She couldn't handle being grilled about it. Her own loss was still far too fresh. Still, she was mindful of the Fifth Commandment, and she figured that she hadn't done an amazing job of honoring her father or her mother so far. She owed it to the woman to at least try.

"What are you planning to do with your life now?" the woman asked, which wasn't at all the way that Rebecca had expected this conversation to go. "Are you going to just stay in your bed and mope forever?"

Rebecca closed her eyes and winced a little. Her mother didn't mean to be unkind. In fact, 'unkind' was pretty much the last word that could be applied to Miriam King. She was, however, matter of fact, pragmatic, and not one to hold back from speaking her mind.

"I know you've lost someone important to you, my child," Miriam said, her tone more gentle. "And I grieve with you. Eli would have made a fine son-in-law. But God has called him home, and you're still here. You're still alive."

Those words sparked something in Rebecca, something that she hadn't felt in quite some time. After a moment, she recognized it as hope. It wasn't a bright, shining hope, like when she'd left with Eli, but it was the hope that maybe her life didn't have to be over.

"I'll help you more," Rebecca promised. She knew that Miriam worked hard, and felt briefly ashamed for her own sadness, which she'd allowed to make her idle. Instead, she would channel it into hard work. "Cleaning, sewing, cooking ... I remember how to do it."

"Do you think," Miriam asked, after a long silence, "That you'll get married?" Her voice was gentle but it still made Rebecca ache inside in a way that she wasn't sure she would ever fully recover from. That wound would never fully heal.

The question was innocuous enough, but they both knew what Miriam was asking. How serious had the relationship been? That wasn't something that Rebecca was willing to discuss with her conservative mother, though.

"Do I have to decide that right now?" Rebecca asked, and her mother reached over and gave her a hug, just a brief one, but one that meant the world to Rebecca. Her mother loved her, that she knew. That meant something, especially since Rebecca knew that she'd put her through a lot.

"No, of course not," Miriam said, and Rebecca nodded. After a brief pause during which she struggled with herself, she gave a soft sigh. It was the right thing to do, even if it wasn't exactly easy for her to do it. Still, she could humble herself, if she had to, and in this case, she did.

"I'm sorry, mother," she said quietly. "I'm sorry for leaving without telling you."

Her words surprised the older woman, she could tell that, but after a long, silent, awkward moment, her mother replied to her.

"And I'm sorry that I didn't fight harder for you and Eli. I always just thought that it was your choice, your decision, but maybe if I'd spoken to his parents ..."

Through the years, Rebecca had had the same thoughts, and hearing them said aloud was comforting. She smiled and hugged her mother again, and with that, she started to move on with her life.

She would never, never forget Eli, she knew that. He would be in her heart forever. But her mother was right. She was still alive, she had her whole life ahead of her, and it was time to start living that life.

It seemed the perfect way to honor Eli's memory, to stay alive and vibrant, just as he had always been.

* * *

For a couple of weeks, it was enough to just stay in the house. She kept remembering the way that Eli's brother had looked at her, and it seemed to her that it was going to be much safer for her to stay away from the general community. The last thing that she wanted was to cause a scene with Eli's family.

Her world, however, had been expanded by her life in the city. At the time, it had been scary, but it had changed her. The walls of her parents' house started to seem more and more restrictive, and eventually, she felt like they were closing in on her.

She wasn't going to be able to sit around in the house all day, sewing and cleaning. She knew what it was like to go out and do something for a living. Her jobs had never been anything special, but she'd felt needed, valued.

The answer to her solution came home with her father one day. He'd been helping one of the other men paint his house, and he walked into the house with big news on his lips.

"Rachel Fisher is getting married."

That was a big deal. Rachel Fisher had been the one and only teacher for many years. Rebecca herself had been instructed in the one room schoolhouse for a couple of years.

Rachel must have been pushing thirty, which was quite the age for a woman to be unmarried, at least in their community. Once she was married, she wouldn't be able to teach. She'd be expected to go take care of her own new family.

All of a sudden, she had it. She knew what she was supposed to be doing, as clear as day. It was almost like someone had spoken the words to her. Like someone had directed her to what she was meant to be doing.

"I will apply for that job."

The sense of rightness only intensified as she said the words. Yes. This was what she was meant to be doing. Even the look that her parents exchanged didn't deflate that sense of purpose in the slightest.

"Rebecca ... That may be difficult, given your past," her father said, his tone doubtful. Rebecca frowned, but listened, leaning forward, the sock that she was darning lying forgotten in her lap.

"I feel like it's what I'm meant to do," Rebecca said. "Yes, I left, but I was called back, don't you see? I can teach the children."

Her father nodded slowly. He was a man of a deep Godliness, and she could tell that her own conviction was swaying him.

"There's a problem, my daughter," Rebecca's mother said, and Rebecca turned to look at her, one eyebrow arched in wordless question. "Amos Fisher."

Instantly, Rebecca understood. The teachers were hired by a committee of three local men, local parents, influential in the community. Somehow, she'd always known that Amos was one of them, but it had never occurred to her to think about what that meant for her before.

Amos Fisher, Rachel's father. Rachel, who was Eli's older sister.

In short, if Rebecca wanted the job, she was going to have to convince a man who hated her that she deserved it.

* * *

Her chance came sooner than she would have imagined.

Rebecca knew that no one thought that she had a chance. Even her own parents, who had been supportive, were sure that she would be frozen out. That there was no chance that Amos would hire her, given his opinion of her.

However, she knew that her own father had told Amos and the other two men that she was interested. Not that she had a lot of hope for that, although she was the most experienced woman who was unmarried. There were very few women of the right age, who had finished school themselves, and of those few, who knew how many were interested?

So when Rebecca went to the dry goods store to get some more cloth for the sewing needs of her family, she was secretly elated to see that Amos was there, too, browsing through some farming implements. This was exactly the sort of meeting that she'd been dreading only a short time ago. Now, however, she couldn't have felt more eager for it.

This was her future that she was fighting for, she reminded herself. Not just because of her wish to be a teacher, but just in general. If she wanted to be accepted, truly accepted, then she was going to have to neutralize Amos.

So, feeling bold, she approached him. It was not something that most of the Amish women would have done, and her insides felt like they were all a-quiver with nerves, but it was necessary.

"Good afternoon," Rebecca said, keeping her voice quiet, but speaking directly to Amos. She kept looking at him, even when it seemed that his first reaction was to simply ignore her, and eventually, he nodded briefly at her, his expression blank.

It wasn't much, but she took it as an encouraging sign.

"I was wondering if you had had a chance to decide who you wish to hire as the new teacher," Rebecca continued, though Amos hardly seemed to be in a talkative mood. Still, it was a fair question, not one that very many people could take offense to.

He, apparently, was an exception to the general rule.

"Not a whore who took my son from me, who got him killed," Amos said, and while Rebecca had tried to keep her voice down, Amos was doing no such thing. He spoke as though inviting the few other patrons of the store to listen to him, to watch as he shamed her. "Not someone who abandoned her people. Why would I bring a viper into a place where children are supposed to learn?"

Rebecca flinched back from him. She wasn't used to being spoken to that way, and a deep, intense, enervating shame filled her. His words were harsh, but were they fair? Hadn't she been the one to get Eli killed?

"You should have stayed in the city," Amos said, and Rebecca felt the blood rush to her cheeks. Suddenly, she felt dizzy, nauseated. "You should have stayed where you belonged, and never darkened the doorsteps of anyone that you betrayed again."

With that, he left, and Rebecca fell back against a display, which was luckily made of strong wood and could support her. Right there, in front of at least ten people, she threw up, closing her eyes against the vertigo and the weakness that threatened to claim her completely.

She had to be helped home by the kind, compassionate daughter of the man who ran the dry goods store.

* * *

Within the next few days, two important things happened.

The first was that Amos and the other men agreed on a teacher to hire, and it wasn't Rebecca. After her run in with the man in the store, she could hardly be surprised by that. She had seen it coming, in all honesty.

The second was much more unexpected. It had been over a month that she'd been back, and she realized, after her disgraceful performance in the store, that during that whole time, she hadn't had her monthly courses even once. Not only that, but her breasts ached, her nipples had darkened, and she felt sick almost all of the time.

After a conversation with her mother that she hoped was discreet enough to keep the older woman in the dark, she had to come to the conclusion that she had been avoiding.

She was with child. With Eli's child. She, an unmarried woman, possibly on her own very soon if her parents decided to kick her out, was going to have a baby.

* * *

The question of how she was going to tell her parents plagued her. She started sleeping more, just as she had when she'd first arrived here, claiming that she had an illness that sapped all of her strength.

It wasn't like that was even inaccurate.

It even occurred to her, as she emptied her stomach once more, holding her hair back from her face, that she could just let nature take its toll. In a few short months, her condition would be obvious to anyone who looked at her. Then she wouldn't have to tell anyone at all.

That's when her mother came in, and when she saw Rebecca crouched down, the older woman sighed and took over the job of holding her hair back.

"How long have you known?" she asked Rebecca, who just shook her head, utterly miserable. Without a word, her mother knew. Of course, she did. Rebecca had hoped otherwise, but it didn't actually surprise her. The woman had been pregnant many times herself, it made perfect sense that she would see the symptoms and recognize them.

"I'm sorry," Rebecca whispered, and she was. All she'd done, it seemed, was bring shame to her family, and she hated that. All she'd wanted to do was follow her heart, but she'd made a mess of all of it.

She had no life ahead of her, and they both knew that without needing to be told. No future at all. She was pregnant, out of wedlock, and she couldn't even marry the father.

"Why did you do it? I thought we taught you better than that." Rebecca's mother's voice was more sad and disappointed than angry, and that, somehow, was far worse.

"It was just once. We were going to get married before we came back," Rebecca said, and then buried her face in her hands and burst into hopeless tears.

It had been bad enough when she'd just been the one who had left and come back. Now she was going to be raising a baby, all on her own. Her parents might even be shunned, utterly ostracized, and she almost certainly would be.

"I wish I'd just stayed, mother," Rebecca said, as she felt her mother's warm, comforting arms wrapping around her, hugging her close. "I wish that I'd married Eli here. That I'd been willing to wait long enough to get his parents' blessing."

Her voice died down, and then, after a long moment, she whispered,

"Maybe then Eli would still be alive."

"Listen to me, Rebecca," her mother said, her tone stern, the voice that Rebecca had always known meant that she was in trouble, that she was being chastised. "I can tell that you think it was your fault. It wasn't. You didn't cause Eli's death."

Rebecca squeezed her eyes against the tears that kept coming, no matter how hard she tried to restrict them. She shook her head. They hadn't even spoken about this, and she was utterly touched by her mother's faith.

Touched, and then even more ashamed, because she was going to have to let her down once more.

"I loved him," Rebecca sobbed, "But I got him killed. He was picking me up from work, mother. He was tired from working his two jobs, but he came to get me so that I could be safe. It was my fault."

Her mother shook her head, her hands warm and comforting on Rebecca's back.

"No, my daughter. That wasn't your fault. Eli did the right thing. It was the fault of the one who caused the accident. I know Eli well enough to know that it couldn't have been him."

Rebecca shook her head. Eli had been driving carefully, as he always did.

"The car ... it came out of nowhere," Rebecca whispered. It hurt to say the words. It hurt to think about it at all. But maybe it was the good kind of hurt, the kind where she was getting rid of something that was festering deep in her soul.

"Any part you had in it, God forgives you, if you repent," Rebecca heard her mother whisper, and the words helped. For the first time, she thought that maybe, just maybe, she could eventually get over what had happened.

With the help of her family, of course, and her Heavenly Father.

* * *

Perhaps it should have tempted her more than it did to go back to the big city. There, no one would even think twice about the fact that she was a single woman with a baby. Sure, there was some stigma around it, but from what she'd seen, it was so common that there was a really good chance that no one would pay much attention.

Besides, she had someone else that she had to think about now. The baby that was, day by day, growing inside her, developing and forming and getting ready to be born. A baby, who was depending on her, above all else.

No. She and Eli had talked about this a great deal. They had never wanted to raise their children in the city. They'd wanted their children to be raised in their faith, in safety, without the bad influences of the city life to impact them.

The temptation wasn't there, not really. Yes, if she left, she wouldn't have to deal with being shamed for what she'd done, what she and Eli had done, but at the same time, there would be so many other problems.

Anyway, it was her actions, and she needed to take responsibility for them. Running away had been a bit of a bad habit for her, and it was a habit that it was time to break.

Even knowing that, however, it took her a good few months to get herself ready for what she knew that she needed to do. Amos Fisher was the grandfather of this child, and he needed to know that she was carrying his son's baby. There was really no other option.

It was terrifying, though. Each and every time she thought about doing it, she felt a deep, painful shame burning in the pit of her very being. She remembered staggering into the wooden display, she remembered the painful bite of it into her lower back, the horrific sensation of everyone looking at her.

Once more, she found herself confined to the house. That suited her just fine, actually. There was always work to do, and slowly, her skill at doing it came back to her.

Along with a surprising sense of satisfaction in the simple tasks. As a child, she'd hated sewing, and cooking, and chafed under the restrictions. As an adult, however, she could lose herself in the rhythms of sewing, and take pride in what she'd made with her own hands, in the satisfaction of feeding her family, in helping.

There was a lot of wisdom to this way of life. It made a lot of sense, and when she was away from the distractions of the city, she found that she had more time to sit back and to just think. To be with herself, to value her interactions with her family.

It was too bad that she would probably be driven out of the community completely once everyone knew that she was pregnant and that she wasn't married to the father.

Day by day, her body changed. At first, it was slow, in almost invisible ways. No one would have noticed, not other than herself. But as the weeks moved on, her stomach, which had been flat and taut, started to gradually round, and she knew that she was running out of time.

Her parents were the only ones that knew. That had been fine when the whole thing had been easily hidden, but what was she supposed to do now that her body was changing? Yes, she could stay hidden in the house, but her family often had visitors, being well respected in the community.

She couldn't hide it forever.

If nothing else, in about five more months, she would have a baby. That would be hard to hide. Not only that, but she wouldn't want her child to have to hide. What sort of life would that be for him or for her? She'd wanted the baby to be raised with the same sort of love and community that she had always felt here.

Besides, she was going to have to carve out some sort of place for her child. There weren't exactly very many children wandering around in this area without both a mother and a father.

It was actually sort of an unknown for her. How people would react, how they would treat her, yes, but also, how they would treat her child, who was blameless in all of this. She just didn't know, and that was utterly terrifying, that made her stomach clench and her heart pound sickeningly.

Still, she knew what she needed to do. In a few short months, her baby would be born, and she had to do her best to make sure there would be a place for them here. Which meant that, as tempting as it was to run or hide, she couldn't do it.

Even knowing that, however, it took a fair bit of time for her to actually come around to doing what needed to be done. Each day, she woke up, determined that that day would be the day. Each day, she ended up deciding that the next day would be better, for one reason or another, none of them entirely made up but neither were they exactly genuine.

It was only when she reached down one morning and felt the gentle curve of her stomach as it started to swell that she realized that she had run out of time. If she didn't go to see Amos, she was risking that someone else would tell him first. Maybe that would be easier on her, but it also wasn't at all fair.

How was she going to bring it up? She agonized over that as she dressed in the clothing that still fit, though only just barely, and modestly covered her braided hair in a white cap. What were the perfect words to use to make the man, who was, she knew, a genuinely good man, understand? Yes, he was a good man, but he was also inflexible, unyielding, maybe even stubborn.

She still didn't know when she left the house, but it didn't matter. Today really was the day, and if she had to make it up as she went along, so be it.

* * *

It was a long walk. Rebecca's parents' farm was big, and while the Fisher family farm was only a few farms away, it was still going to take her a couple of hours to walk that distance. Not only was it fairly far, since all of the farms were relatively large, but she wasn't moving all that quickly these days.

Though her energy was coming back, she noticed. The early days of her pregnancy had left her exhausted. She wouldn't be sad to leave that behind.

Still, even after the walk, she arrived at the farm, still having no idea what to say. Which she couldn't let stop her from walking up to the front porch and squaring her shoulders before knocking.

Amos himself, who must have been in for lunch, opened the door. His look of polite inquiry transformed itself into anger immediately, and he opened his mouth, no doubt to say something cutting, to send her away.

She couldn't let that happen.

All of her half-formed plans flew out of her head, and she looked him directly in the eye and ended up just blurting the words out.

"I'm with child. In five months, I will have Eli's baby."

There. It was out. The words that she'd been tormenting herself over how to say, they were out there in the open. It had been her obligation, to Eli and to his family, to say them, and now, she had.

There was a long, long silence, and then Amos nodded. It was impossible for her to know what he was thinking. He'd never been the sort of man to talk about his emotions all that much. The one exception that she could think of was when he'd gotten so angry at the store.

Not a good thing for her to think about.

"Who is it, Amos?" a woman's voice called. A familiar voice. It was Charity Fisher, Eli's mother.

"It's Rebecca King," Amos said, and his voice cracked, just the tiniest bit, on the last syllable. "She's brought us news."

Charity came out, standing beside her husband, looking at Rebecca with curiosity, just faintly tinged with hostility. Charity had never been quite as displeased with Rebecca as Amos had, but doubtless, she wasn't her biggest fan ever since Rebecca had run off with Eli.

Rebecca took a deep breath, and she almost reached out to take Charity's hand. The grandmother of her child, of Eli's child. She wanted to touch her, to form some sort of link, but in the end, she didn't quite dare.

"I'm pregnant," she said softly. "Please, don't ... I just thought that you should know. That you both should know. You're going to be grandparents."

To her surprise, Rebecca saw tears in Charity's eyes. Amos still wasn't saying anything, but Charity, acting apparently on an impulse, reached out and did what Rebecca hadn't quite dared to do. She took Rebecca's hands and squeezed them.

"What wonderful news," Charity said, and her voice was much more emotional. Her fingers, when they grasped Rebecca, were tight and her hands were shaking just a little bit.

Charity missed Eli just as much as Rebecca did, she realized with wonder. This whole time, she'd been living alone with her grief, when there was a woman right here who could have potentially shared that with her.

If only Rebecca had been brave enough to reach out to her, and not just Amos, before.

"We were never married," Rebecca ventured hesitantly. She hated to bring it up, but she didn't want there to be any more lying, any more hiding things or secrets, between them.

Charity nodded.

"It doesn't matter," the older woman said. "As of this day, you are my daughter. I will help you to raise the child, and so, I know, will your mother."

It was unconventional, to be sure, but then, the whole situation was. Maybe it didn't have to be the tragedy that she'd always assumed it would be, however. Maybe, just maybe, things could work out for her.

"I'll need the help," Rebecca said, laughing through the tears in her own eyes, the ones that mirrored Chastity's. "And you have the experience." Chastity had, after all, given birth to a dozen children. She knew what she was doing.

With this woman, she knew that her baby would be safe. She knew that Chastity, once she'd decided that a child was hers, would defend it until the end.

She had no doubt at all that the woman would do the same for her grandchild, as well.

Slowly, Rebecca, still holding Chastity's hands, looked over at Amos, who had yet to say much of anything. Who was standing there, staring at her?

She'd won over Chastity, perhaps. Or the baby had, anyway, which was good enough. What of Amos, though? She watched him, just waiting. Could he unbend enough to allow her into his life, for the sake of his son? For the sake of his son's child?

For a moment, the tension stretched between them, and Rebecca became more and more sure that he would make her leave. That he would hurl cruel words at her, just as he had in the store. He wasn't the sort of man that would normally give up a grudge, not when his anger was righteous.

"God forgive me," Amos said suddenly, and to her surprise, she saw that his eyes were suspiciously shiny, as well, like he might be holding back some emotions of his own. "I drove you away."

"I forgive you if you will do the same for me," Rebecca nodded, and Amos considered that for a long moment before nodding.

"Welcome to the Fisher family, Rebecca," he said, finally saying the words that were all that she'd wanted to hear for so long.

She had a home, and so did her baby.

They would be safe.

The End

Samuel and Greta

MICELLE MANN

Samuel

Samuel wiped the sweat from his brow and sat back on his heels to admire his handiwork. The crib was one of beauty and while simplistically crafted, the miniscule detail was a credit to his attention. *I hope the Chandlers will be happy with this,* Samuel thought to himself, rising to his feet with agility but even as he thought it, he knew that they would be more than content with his latest project. The Chandler family had been customers of the Bender family for generations and even after Samuel's father had passed the previous spring, the Chandlers had continued to use Samuel as their carpenter despite his young age and relative inexperience.

"I understand if you would rather use another craft man, Mrs. Chandler," Samuel had said not long after his father's death. "I haven't nearly business which my father had."

Miriam Chandler had shaken her head vehemently.

"Oh no, Samuel! Carpentry is in your blood. You are an artists and artists don't need to paint a thousand pictures to be wonderful. You are a natural. My family will continue to use you and I am certain that the others on the community feel the same as I do. Do not fret, child. You and yours will not be forsaken during this time."

"I appreciate the sentiment, Mrs. Chandler but we will be fine," Samuel said with a slight twinge of anger. He did not want the pity of his congregation. *They see us a charity mission,* he had thought but the reality was, despite their newly orphaned status, the Bender children were very well revered in their small Pennsylvania district. Samuel genuinely was a gifted tradesman, something his father had done very well to ensure from the time the boy was young. Mrs. Chandler had not been fibbing; Samuel had a natural talent for working with wood. It went deeper than his ability to work with his hands. He had an affinity with the trees and could often be found wandering through the gullies when the long work day was completed. It was not uncommon to see him conversing with the long-standing beasts, explaining the plans he had for them, how much good they would be doing for the people in the future. Samuel was a gentle soul and it reflected in everything he did. He was the second oldest child in his family and while his oldest sister Greta tended to their small animal farm, Samuel was afforded some freedom to earn extra wages with his woodworking. The two youngest children, Zachariah and Sadie were still in school however, after the death of their father, they had made themselves indispensable to their oldest siblings handling light chores and cooking. It was God's blessing that their aunt and uncle lived moments away via carriage and often offered their assistance with the youngest children. *We are so fortunate to live in such a place where death brings us closer rather than tearing us apart.* When Samuel's father had taken ill, both the family and community had bound together and helped prepare the siblings for the inevitable. The road had been painful and slow but by the time the oldest living Bender had succumbed to his fate at the young age of forty-seven, leaving behind four mourning children. Regardless of the hardships they had endured, their relationship had thrived and grown as a result.

"Samuel! Samuel, are you out here?" Greta's voice piped through the workshop and Samuel turned to face his sister. She rounded the corner and looked at him.

"Yes, Greta. Is all well?"

"Yes, supper is ready. I just wanted to make sure that you didn't lose track of time again. Yesterday you stayed here well into the night working and didn't eat a morsel."

"I just want to make sure that this cradle is perfect for the Chandlers," Samuel protested, standing back so his older sister could see his completed project. She nodded admiringly but put her hands on her hips disapprovingly.

"It looks lovely but that is no excuse for poor diet. Zachariah and Sadie depend on you and we can't afford for you to become ill. You must be more conscious of how much you are eating. You will fade away if you are not careful."

Samuel laughed and followed Greta out of the small structure, wiping his hands on his slacks.

"I don't think there's any fear of that," he replied but he understood her concern. He was losing weight on his already slight frame. Greta grunted.

"Don't laugh, Samuel. It isn't funny. *Daed* lost a lot of weight when he got sick, remember? It makes the younger ones worry about you."

Startled, Samuel stopped in his tracks.

"What a terrible thing to say, Greta! I am not sick!"

"I know you're not but Sadie and Zachariah make the connection that you are losing weight as papa did. They are young and it makes them worry. You spend far too much time in the woods and not enough time caring for yourself."

Slowly, Samuel nodded and continued walking after her toward their modest home. *She is right. She will be married soon and I will be left to care for them alone when she moves to another district. I must be more aware of how they see me.* As they approached the house, Sadie met them at the back door, bouncing from one foot to the other in excitement.

"What is it, Sadie?" Samuel asked with some alarm. Her small face broke into a beam.

"Nothing!" she squealed. "The Chandlers had their baby! A little boy! And they named him after you, Samuel!"

A feeling of warmth and happiness swept over Samuel. He shot Greta a glance and they grinned at each other.

"Now you see? It's a good thing I stayed up late to finish the crib." Greta shook her head begrudgingly.

"Wait! Where are you going?" she demanded as Samuel turned back toward the workshop.

"Didn't you hear Sadie? The Chandlers had their baby and named him after me! I can't have them waiting for their cradle or they'll regret their decision!"

"Samuel! Not before you eat! Samuel!" But her younger brother was already halfway across the property, either ignoring or unhearing Greta's pleas. *I must rush this over to the Chandlers right away! I hope it does not disappoint them. I wonder if one day I will make one like this for my own children. Maybe I should think about finding a mother for those children first.* Samuel chuckled to himself, his smile overtaking his face. As he hurried into the shed, his heart bursting with pride and elation, he did not notice the figure standing behind under the giant pine, watching him in the gentle hue of twilight.

Willa

She ducked swiftly as the glass flew directly at her head and tried to steady her trembling hands before she slowly turned. Her father's rage stained face glowered at her from across the table.

"You will sit down this instant!" Seth Albrecht was incensed but Willa was long accustomed to these violent outbursts.

"I will return when you have calmed," she answered with a nonchalance she did not possess. Her heart hammering, she quickly walked out the door, expecting a blow to reach her before she had a chance to exit the room but it did not materialize. Willa hurried toward the ravine at the rear of the property. How Seth handled her perceived insolence would vary from day to day. Some days he would allow for her to leave without incident whereas other times, removing herself from the situation would result in a fate worse than death. On occasions when Seth did not follow, Willa would return home as if there had not been a dramatic scene mere hours before and he would be the same loving, doting father whom she had adored since childhood and she would eagerly accept his good mood. But the dreaded times when he did chase after her, she knew that it was in her best interest to stay away for the night for once she returned home, the beating would be merciless and no amount of pleading or cajoling would help.

As she reached the outskirt of the gulley, she paused behind a coniferous tree to glance back at the house and exhaled in relief. Seth had not come outside. She would be safe to go home that night. The previous week she had spent the night in the Flickinger barn where Mr. Flickinger had discovered her in the morning. He had shooed her out of the horse stall with a pitchfork as though she was a diseased hobo, ripe to rob him blind. Willa had grown up in the district with these people and attended worship with their sons and daughters but she was not one of them. Willa was the only child of Seth and Sara Albrecht. Her father was a candlemaker and her mother a seamstress, often catering to the English. Willa was afforded many luxuries which some of her peers were not such as a toy chest filled with handmade dolls and more outfits than the other girls in the district. It wasn't long before the Albrechts were being reprimanded for spoiling young Willa.

"You must think of having siblings for her. She is becoming too good for the other children. You can see it in the way she acts," the Bishop warned them when Willa was five. The bishop did not understand that Sara had taken extreme caution not to produce more children with her husband in fear for their safety. Instead, Sara had curtly told him that Willa was not spoiled and if the other children felt inadequate, it was the fault of their parents and not of the Albrecht parenting. After that, the Albrechts became outcasts in their own home. No one had any idea what was occurring behind closed doors and in fact, Seth was often regarded as the victim in the circumstance.

"That poor man. Married to a shrew who treats their daughter like an English princess," the gossips would say behind their backs. "He shouldn't allow for Sara to spend so much time in town doing work for those people. It is affecting their way of life."

The members of the community did not see the bruises on Sara and Willa's bodies as Seth rarely struck in the face and they spent so little time paying mind to the women that the signs of domestic abuse were lost upon them. It was easier to disregard the women as uppity than to delve deeper into the true story. When Willa was thirteen, Sara abruptly disappeared. At first, Willa was certain that Seth had murdered her but there was absolutely no proof to that effect. Willa desperately tried to find evidence that he had harmed her mother but as a year passed, Willa was forced to realize that her mother had simply had enough and had fled. Seth fell into the role of abandoned husband with sociopathic ease and relished the attention which the district bestowed upon him. He gobbled down their sympathy with humbleness, accepting the outpouring as if he deserved it. It was around this time that Willa realized that her father was not of sound reasoning. The eligible women made it clear that they were there for him, bringing meals and cleaning his home. Their brazenness made Willa sick to her stomach, especially when she knew what kind of man they were pursuing. She was still young enough to believe if she spoke, she would be heard and she desperately tried to forewarn everyone about Seth. Of course, she was again regarded as mean spirited and disregarded.

"What kind of cruel child says such awful things about their own father when he is going such a trying time? This is what happens when you spare the rod," the community squawked. Little did they know that when Seth caught wind of his daughter's warnings, the rod was not spared, not in the least. The beatings became more and more intense but with every blow, Willa grew stronger somehow, against the odds. When Willa turned fourteen, Rose Slagel began spending more and more time at the Albrecht home and the teenager knew that she could not stand to watch the naïve, idealistic Rose become Seth's next victim. It did not help that Rose genuinely wanted to befriend Willa. The younger girl knew that any attempt to dissuade Rose from becoming ensnared in Seth's trap would be an exercise in futility. So, with a heart filled with fear, Willa packed a small bag and followed in her mother's footsteps one night, disappearing without a trace. Her brave journey took her into the big city where she lived on the streets for several months, begging for money. There were several options for a young, innocent girl in a morally bankrupt world but Willa managed to scrape by without resorting to any form of activity shunned by God. When the weather turned bitter, Willa's homespun clothing and little street smarts did nothing to protect her from the concrete jungle. The people became more aggressive with the cold, recognizing their own survival at stake. Her safety was compromised constantly and fifteen-year-old Willa was in a constant internal battle with herself. *Is this better or worse than living with father? Am I more or less safe here? Where will I die first?* The need for food and shelter won out and with her tail between her legs, she was forced to return home. Seth allowed her but only if she was baptized immediately. Malnourished, friendless and out of options, Willa agreed. Following the baptism, she was severely beaten and starved for three days. Seth forced her to sleep in the woodshed all three of those nights without a blanket. She would have been warmer on the streets and likely better fed also.

A few years passed and Willa continued to endure the abuse by the hands of her father, unbeknown to anyone, including Rose Slagel whom Seth had married in Willa's absence. It gave Willa some relief to know that Rose was safe from Seth but she often wondered why. The answer came when Rose announced her pregnancy at the end of the second year. Soon after the baby was born, a premature girl, that Rose began to receive the same treatment. *He wants a son!* Willa finally realized.

"Willa, you must leave here. I will get you some money. You are young and have your entire life ahead of you. But you must leave this place," Rose urged her one morning after Seth had left for his workshop. Willa had snorted contemptuously.

"Oh? And where will I go? I almost died on the street once. Why don't you go? It isn't too late for baby Lucy."

"I cannot leave here. I have my family. Lucy needs her father."

"And I don't need my father, Rose?" Willa shot back furiously. She knew she was being unreasonable, that her step-mother was trying to protect her but she suddenly was just as angry at Rose as she was at Seth. *Why didn't she just listen to me? Why didn't they just all stay away?* She thought mournfully. It was too late. Seth had claimed another victim.

As Willa wound her way through the very familiar pathway, she started to wonder if Rose was right. Perhaps she should leave. There was nothing in the community for her. Her skills as a seamstress were mediocre and she was not apt to be married as she was a pariah in the district. She had no friends, no family. She desperately wished she knew where her mother had gone but of course there was no way to find that out without money, money which she did not have. Willa turned toward the Bender farm and stopped by Samuel's workshop. Willa peered inside and saw that no one was inside. Content, she leaned heavily against the huge pine overhanging the small structure and dug into her apron pocket. Her hands closed around a tin which she pulled out. Inside the nondescript case were two hand rolled cigarettes and a pack of matches. Immediately, she lit one and inhaled deeply. The sun was beginning to set and Willa felt her stomach grumble. Seth had started just as they were to sit down to dinner meaning that Willa was going to spend another evening without food. Suddenly she heard a voice call out.

"Samuel! Not before you eat! Samuel!" Willa dropped the cigarette and ducked behind the tree as Samuel Bender came striding confidently toward her hiding spot, a serene smile on his beautiful face. Willa felt a pang as she looked upon his face. Samuel had always been one of the few people in the community who had been kind to her despite her wretched reputation. If she had thought it possible, Willa would have believed that she had a deep seeded affection for the man. *Well if there was anyone in this district I could care for, I imagine it would be Samuel Bender,* she told herself, watching with relief as he opened the door to the woodshed, apparently not seeing her. Willa waited, unmoving until he walked out a moment later, a wooden cradle in his arms. Willa felt her heart begin to quicken as an obscure thought crossed through her mind. *I wonder if he will make one of those for our children.* Before she could stop herself, Willa fully exposed herself and called out.

"Samuel!"

<u>Greta</u>

"You seem elsewhere, Greta. Is everything all right?" Ivan peered at his fiancée but she did not seem to hear him. Her hazel eyes were focussed on her brother, her stomach churning with some unidentifiable emotion.

"Greta!" She jumped and looked at Ivan.

"Dear Lord, Ivan, I am sitting right here. No need to scream in my ear!" she admonished as she took his arm. They rose from the sitting room and headed outside to join the rest of the congregation.

"I tried speaking to you normally but apparently, you seem to have selective hearing. Why are you staring at Samuel like that?" Greta narrowed her eyes.

"Like what?" she denied. Ivan laughed and shrugged.

"Don't play coy with me, *liebchen*. I can see the way you're staring at your brother. What is going on? Are you quarrelling?"

Again, Greta stared at Ivan as though he were crazy.

"Quarreling? With Samuel? Over what?" she demanded. Ivan shook his head.

"I agree, it seems to be a rather odd question as Samuel is hardly one to give you any trouble but I can't help but sense that something is wrong. What is it?"

"That's just it – I'm not sure," Greta confessed, lowering her voice, her eyes trained on Samuel once more. Zachariah and Sadie were at his side and Samuel seemed to be entertaining them and other children with a captivating tale.

"What do you mean?" Ivan pressed. Greta chose her words carefully, trying not to sound outlandish.

"He has been acting slightly...different," she said slowly.

"Different how?"

"I don't know...I can't pinpoint it exactly but there's something evasive about him as of late."

"You have to be more specific, Greta. *You're* starting to sound evasive," Ivan joked.

Greta shook her head and sighed.

"Ever since the night the Chandler baby was born, he has been acting secretive. For example, he says he is out working in his shed and then I go to call on him and he's in the shed but he's not working on anything. He's just standing there guiltily." Ivan blinked.

"Maybe he just needs a break from everyone," he offered. "I can understand that."

"Perhaps," Greta agreed. "But I can't shake the sense that he is hiding something."

"Maybe he is courting someone," Ivan said flippantly but Greta nodded, looking grim.

"That's what I'm afraid of," she confirmed.

"Why? He's of an age where marriage should be on his mind," Ivan told her reprovingly. Greta sighed.

"I agree. I'm not concerned that he courting someone. My concern is who he is courting."

Greta had discovered Samuel's secret by accident. Zachariah had been sent home from school due to a fever and Greta needed Samuel to watch over the boy while she tended to the vegetables. She could not find her brother in the shed as he had promised to be but instead discovered him in the woods. This was not unusual but aside from the rare red in Samuel's cheeks, there was a fresh cigarette butt on the ground by his feet.

"Are you smoking?" Greta had almost screamed at him. Samuel shook his head vehemently.

"Of course, not!" Samuel had retorted. "What do you want?"

Taken aback by his tone, Greta had looked around in the trees, suddenly sensing that they were not alone.

"Who is out here with you?" she demanded.

"No one," Samuel had answered quickly, covering the space between them. He led his older sister out of the trees.

"Zach is home sick. I need you to tend to him," she told him, looking over her shoulder. She saw nothing but the sense of unease did not disappear. Over the following days, Samuel's behavior became more furtive and Greta's maternal instinct grew shaper. It was not until a week later that Greta finally made sense of what her brother may be hiding. Rose Albrecht appeared on the Bender farm looking troubled.

"Hello, Greta. Is Samuel home?" Rose asked, baby Lucy asleep in her arms. Greta rose from the vegetable garden, her brow furrowed.

"I believe he is in the work shed, Mrs. Albrecht. Is there something I can do for you?"

"I am looking for Willa," the new mother said worriedly. "She has not been home in three days."

Greta felt the blood drain from her face.

"Well I assure you, that girl would not be here," Greta stated indignantly. "Why would you think such a thing?"

Rose's mouth pursed into a line and she reached into her apron pocket. She held out her hand and Greta drew near to see what she held.

"I found this in Willa's room," Rose said simply. Greta took the item and saw it was a hand wooden rose. The workmanship was definitely that of Samuel and Greta could not reconcile the meaning.

"No, I don't think that is a very good idea," Willa mumbled, again retreating into the trees.

"Wait! Don't leave, Willa. I – why don't you stay here in my shed. I won't be long. Unless you have to get home?"

Gratefully, Willa looked at him and nodded eagerly.

"I can wait!" she exclaimed. "I don't need to be home."

Samuel was consumed with a bittersweet feeling. He had a feeling that Willa was in no rush to get home but he was happy she would be there when he returned. True to his word, he was back in less than an hour and Willa was waiting for him by the light of a single kerosene lamp. They spent that night talking into the wee hours of the morning with Samuel sneaking back into the house before Greta woke at dawn. He had no illusions about what his sister would say if she discovered he was hiding Willa Albrecht in his workshop. The following morning, Samuel hurried back into the shed. He was filled with a deep disappointment that Willa had left. He wondered where she had gone. *If she went home, will Seth be angry with her? Will he harm her?* In his distress, Samuel absently picked up a small piece of wood and began to whittle. As his mind turned, his hands created. The morning light spilled into afternoon heat and when Greta appeared at the door to the shop, Samuel dropped the piece into his pocket guiltily.

"What are you doing, Samuel?" she demanded, looking around suspiciously.

"Working," Samuel barked with more anger than he intended.

"On what?"

"What is it, Greta?"

"You are acting strangely. Come inside and eat."

After supper, Willa was back outside the trees as if she was silently willing him to return. She did not know what she was doing there. The previous night, she had left slightly after Samuel had snuck back into the house, wondering what nightmare she was facing in her own home. To her surprise, the family was sound asleep and no one had missed her.

Seth had left for his shed in the morning and Rose had waited for her to wake.

"You must consider leaving here," Rose told her again as she fed Lucy. A flash of annoyance sparked through Willa's body.

"You cannot get rid of me that easily, Rose," Willa retorted, ignoring her step-mother's distressed look.

"You can fight me, Willa or you can heed the advice of someone older and wiser than you. You cannot stay out all night long and not expect there to be serious consequences. Last night I managed to talk him down. Tonight, you may not be so lucky."

"Oh? Am I lucky?" Willa laughed but worry flooded her belly. A small part of her wondered still if Seth had anything to do with Sara's disappearance even though she knew logically that her mother had simply had enough one day. Every day Willa wondered if Seth would go too far. Rose's words only reiterated something she often considered. Willa left the house that afternoon and waited in the woods for Samuel to appear. When he finally did, he led her inside the shed and placed something in her hand. When she opened her hand, it was a hand carved wooden rose. The detail was so akin to the one that Samuel's father had made her years previous that it brought Willa to her knees with melancholy. They spent the evening side by side in the woodshed, their fingers gently tracing circles in each other's palms. Slightly after midnight, Samuel escorted Willa back to her home. Before she scampered off into the dark house, Samuel grabbed her arm.

"Are you certain you're safe?" he asked, staring deeply into her eyes. She looked away and nodded, glancing at the still, dark building. Impulsively, he leaned over and kissed her. Surprised she jolted back. They looked at each other and then Willa beamed. She leaned forward and deposited another sweet kiss on his lips and disappeared into the darkness. Smiling, Samuel headed toward his own home. As Willa quietly crept into the silent kitchen, a blow hit her face without warning.

"Where have you been?" Seth hissed. Shocked, Willa's hand flew to her face.

"I w-was out for a walk," she breathed, backing away.

"Are you acting like a fallen woman? Trolling around in the night?" he hissed, drawing closer to her. Another fist hit her in the stomach and Willa doubled over, gasping.

"Seth! Leave her be!" Rose yelled, running down the stairs.

"You get back to bed and mind your own!" Seth snarled. Willa took the distraction as an opportunity to flee the house, Seth screaming with rage. As she fumbled off into the woods, she saw him lumbering after her in the pale moonlight but Willa knew he would never catch her. She knew the woods much better than he ever would. Rose stood on the landing, trembling, tears streaking her face. On the floor by the bottom step lay an intricate wooden rose pendant.

"Are you chasing after a fallen woman?"

Samuel froze in his tracks as Greta's voice rang out in the darkness.

"Fallen woman?" he asked innocently without turning around.

"Look at me when I am speaking to you, Samuel," Greta snapped.

Samuel spun on his heel and stared back at his sister.

"Why in God's name would you pick Willa Albrecht of all the eligible women in our district, Samuel? You have the world at your feet! You are handsome, intelligent, patient! She is trouble!"

"You don't know anything about Willa, Greta!"

"I know she smokes cigarettes, even though she is baptized and has sworn to follow God's will. I know that she lived on the streets doing God knows what with God knows who. I know she lies and I know she was arrested while fraternizing with the English."

"Oh you *know* these things, do you?"

"Don't be facetious, Samuel. I care about you and I will not have you hitch your star to a wagon not worthy of your time." Samuel was suddenly furious.

"No matter how much you pretend to be, you are not my mother, Greta. I am a man who can decide whom I will or will not marry."

"Marry?" Greta's mouth dropped open. "You cannot marry that woman!"

"That woman has a name. Her name is Willa. Please use it from now on." Without waiting for a response, Samuel ran up the stairs, his heart racing. It was out of character for him to fight with Greta but Willa was a sensitive topic. *Greta doesn't understand Willa is a beautiful person. Inside and out.*

The following morning, he discovered Willa asleep under the pine by the wood shop. He saw the bruise around her eye and she did not leave the shed again for three days. Samuel brought her food and water and stayed with her as often as possible, managing to keep her from Greta's prying eyes. On the third day, Samuel convinced her to go into the woods with him. He showed her how to speak to the trees and she found herself more enamored with him than she had been prior. It was then that they had overheard Rose and Greta in the garden. Samuel pulled her back into the trees.

"We will wait here," he told her, holding her close but Willa shook her head.

"No. I am tired of running," she told him and Samuel looked down at her in surprise.

"You don't have to come, Samuel. I will not embarrass you in front of Greta. I will say I snuck into your shed and stayed here without your knowledge." Samuel scowled.

"You will do no such thing. You are not someone I am ashamed to be with. If you are ready to come forward, I am at your side."

"You will face a lot of backlash, Samuel," Willa warned him.

"You are going to be my wife. There is nothing we can't face together," he answered, hugging her tightly. She stared up at him in disbelief.

"You want to marry me?" she whispered.

"More than anything in the world."

They smiled at one another.

"Are you ready?" Willa nodded and together they headed back toward the shed. They almost collided with Willa's stepmother and Samuel's sister.

"Oh Samuel," Greta's voice was leaden with disappointment. "What are you doing?"

"It's not his fault, Greta," Willa piped in. "I – "

"Willa has been staying in the woodshop," Samuel interrupted.

"Why would you allow for this, Samuel?" Greta asked, shaking her head angrily.

"Because Seth is abusive." Greta snorted.

"Oh, Samuel you are so gullible. She is making up stories for pity," Greta snapped, glaring at Willa. Willa hung her head, tears welling in her eyes. She felt as though she was thirteen years old again and being judged by the entire community, being called a liar.

"No, she's not." Rose spoke for the first time, drawing closer to her stepdaughter. She gently reached out and touched her yellowing eye. Willa drew away.

"Seth hits Willa and I frequently. Sara left because of his abuse." Greta and Willa stared at Rose open mouthed.

"I came to find you, Willa because I went to the authorities in town today and filed a police report. They have arrested your father and I need you to testify. I am worried for Lucy," Rose continued. "Will you please come with me? I have had enough for all of us."

Tears spilled onto Willa's cheeks and she choked on the emotions she was feeling. It was a heady feeling to be believed for the first time in her life.

"Yes! Oh yes!" She threw her arms around Rose who returned her embrace with intensity.

"I'm sorry it took so long. I should have protected you better. But it isn't too late for us." Willa nodded, brushing the tears from her face. She turned to look at her fiancé, her face filled with love.

"Thank you for believing in me," she said as she followed Rose.

"You are my wife-to-be. I will always believe in you," he replied. Rose smiled at the words and Greta stood, silently dumbfounded at the revelations she had just learned. As Rose and Willa walked away, Rose grabbed for Willa's hand and placed the pendant in her palm.

CHOOSING LOVE

ANNABELLE CROWLEY

It was a beautiful Sunday, and Bridget woke at the sound of the crowing rooster. The sun filtered through the curtains like warm liquid, and splashed Bridget's face with a welcome warmth. There were still hours left until church, and Bridget stretched luxuriously in bed, smiling. Then suddenly - a loud crash. Bridget's smile fell. The children were awake.

Bridget lived in a sturdy Amish house that her great-grandfather had built in the 70's, with her father and six siblings. Her mother had died in childbirth leaving Bridget, the oldest, to take care of the domestic affairs while the younger boys helped their father in the fields. She sighed. She hated when the children woke before her.

"Good morning, Papa," she said cheerfully as she entered the living room fully dressed, her plain clothes firmly secured with hooks and pins, hair pulled back in a modest bun. Her father grunted in reply, staring down at a handwritten letter.

Bridget worriedly noted the gray tinge to his face - he'd been getting sicker and sicker. Last month he nearly collapsed, clutching his heart. But the village doctor passed away almost four months ago, and his apprentice, a fourteen year old boy, had almost killed the little Bram baby by forgetting to wash his cut before dressing it.

Bridget stoked the fire while her sisters played with straw dolls on the floor. She scolded one of them, "Lydia, stop that foolishness and get me a bucket of water."

Bridget's father looked up from the letter and chuckled. "You sound like your mother when you talk to that girl."

"Maybe it's because she reminds me of myself," replied Bridget wistfully, watching the her little girl with long briads scamper to the well.

A sudden rumble sounded from above the road, Bridget cursed under her breath and then winced, hoping her father hadn't heard. He looked at her sharply, but said nothing - just a warning this time, then.

"It's those Robinsons," he explained, "those traitors and their tourists."

The Robinsons were a young family of terrible farmers; their crops died on the vine, every year. To supplement their income, they had begun riding their buggy to the nearby city (more a town, really), picking up elementary schoolers and their teachers for educational field trips. This was widely seen as the most disastrous sort of betrayal. No one could bear the thought of those godless children, with their grimy bare hands, touching the Robinsons' prized cows, churning their butter, picking their corn.

Bridget clucked her tongue, "I swear their milk will go sour while it's still in the cow if they go on like this."

"Some people are shameless," agreed her father.

"Sister Bridget?" a voice piped in. It was Lydia, precariously shouldering the cauldron full of water. "I think there's something wrong with Bessie, she keeps licking her shoulder."

"I'll look at it after breakfast," Bridget said.

The oatmeal bubbled over the fire and the children lined up with their wooden bowls.

"We're getting a new doctor," Paul said, looking almost nervous.

Bridget frowned. Something was up - her father was a strong man, a farmer and a good man. He had saved the farm from the brink of destruction by financial ruin and poor weather many a time. She had rarely seen him look as unsure as he did at that moment. She raised one eyebrow.

"And? Anyone we know?"

"It's Amos," answered Paul grimly, and Bridget felt the ground under her rumble. Her vision flattened into a thin circle, and she swallowed nervously.

"I thought he was done with us. He thought we were *backwards*. That he needed to get out. That he..." she trailed off.

"That he would rather die than marry an Amish girl," finished Paul. The details of that infamous last line had resounded through the town, and even now, five years later, remained fresh in everyone's mind.

"So he's really coming back?"

"Yes," confirmed Paul. "Listen, Bridget-"

"I know what you're going to say."

"There are a lot of eligible young men in the town. Adam, Gabriel, all fine, strong men who would love and provide for you. Amos may be settling back here now, but don't forget that he left the church, he left the people who needed him. He left you."

"I know, Papa," Bridget frowned for a second. "But I think you should go to him, when he comes."

Paul opened his mouth as if to argue, when a deep hacking cough emerged from the back of his throat.

"I'll go to him, Bridget, I'll let him fix me up. But that doesn't mean I trust him."

After that, there was no more talk of Amos. Together, the children, Bridget, and Paul ate their oatmeal which was mixed with brown sugar and huckleberries. The little wood chime that Lydia had made tinkled enchantingly in the spring breeze. The corn was rising from the ground in tender shoots, the cows were healthy and full of milk to be pumped from ripe udders. Down the road, Bridget knew, were many handsome, well-mannered men who were clamoring to talk to her, dance with her, maybe even give her a chaste kiss on the hand or lips.

It was a beautiful, perfect morning in a beautiful, perfect life.

Bridget wasn't about to let Amos ruin it for her.

By the time Bridget got her sisters and brothers ready for church, wrangling the boys into starch collared shirts, the girls into long cotton dresses, they were almost late.

"Hurry *up*, Bridget," Paul tapped his foot impatiently. Even with his straw hat drawn low and his collar pulled up severely around his chin, he looked weak, sickly. Bridget had a brief moment of intense fear as she looked at him. "*Bridget*," he scolded, and she snapped out of it.

She ferried the children out the door, and they piled into the carriage while Bridget and her father sat up front. Bridget drove, holding the whip - unconventional, yes, but with her father's weakening muscles, the family had no choice.

The church was tall and white, built and rebuilt by the hands of many generations working together. Today, it was strung with flowers - it is the first day of fall, and the town was celebrating.

"So good to see you," said Paul to the passing Maribel family, who were huffing on foot because their horse had thrown a hoof. A young man, sweetly handsome, caught Bridget's eyes and smiled warmly but demurely. Bridget looked away, flattered; Eliot was the most eligible bachelor in town.

After tying their horses to the picket fence, Bridget and her family lined into the pew, and settled in to listen to the sermon. Father Mathews was a gentle speaker, far more sweet-spoken than most speakers. Bridget was somewhat sinfully in the habit of letting his voice carry her into the fields, away from the substance of the sermon and into a welcoming half-sleep.

"We must be conscious of the beauty around us, for beauty is not something to be squandered. Beauty is God's gift, and we must never let it go without seeking to return."

Bridget became aware of a rustling on the other side of the pew. A man was turning and looking at her. This was met with a ripple of frowns throughout the congregation - these were people who had mastered stillness. Bridget looked out of the corner of her eye at the sudden movement.

Amos; thick brown hair that swept in curls over his forehead, high cheekbones, a chin with the strength of earth. He had become handsomer, more of a man, with thick dark stubble around his lip and beard, and what seemed like an additional layer of strength and muscle over his already tall and strong body.

Amos. Bridget saw herself as he might see her; red-haired as always, with wide hips and a healthy bust, a face peppered with child-like freckles. The same as always, if a bit more exhausted. She squirmed in her seat.

"...And we welcome back into our midst the young Amos, who has seen the error of his ways and has returned once more to his community, his family. Have you anything to say, Amos?"

And Bridget watched as he turned his gaze away from her and spoke loud and clear to the congregation: "I left thinking that I had no need of the things that made me who I am; the friends, hard work, and devotion to God that I was raised with, that raised me. I return now, to offer my services as a man of medicine. I may not have acquired my skills through honest, Amish ways, but I hope that I can save at least one life, and through that life become closer to the God I abandoned."

There was some impressed raising of eyebrows at this. The boy spoke well. Lydia, sitting besides Bridget, hissed, "he speaks like a city boy," but she was the only one who was unimpressed. Bridget felt her past and her grievances fall into the well of Amos' words. Amos, who she once knew so well.

After the church, the entire congregation headed to the yard for butter, bread and cheese, spread out on long linen tables. Because it was first fall, the church had also slaughtered a cow, and the smell of fat hitting the fire began to waft into the air.

Bridget rushed through the busy, happy, bodies, trying to find her father.

"Aren't you staying?" asked a voice, concerned.

"Oh, I..." answered Bridget, before rushing away. When she found her father, she half collided with him.

"Can we *go*?" she asked, seething.

Paul looked at his daughter one moment, the anxiety that peppered her unknowingly beautiful face. "In a moment, baby."

Bridget winced. Paul only called her baby when he was particularly worried about her, or when he thought she had been overworked. He sidestepped her gently and walked towards Farmer Gibbons, with whom he was negotiating a deal for a new horse.

She stood there for a long minute, staring at the spring time joy on people's faces, and feeling utterly and completely alone.

Then, suddenly, a hand on her shoulder. Bridget spun around and looked up into the face of - she wasn't even surprised - Amos.

"Listen, Bridget," he paused. Against her better judgement, she looked up at the full force of his face. His face looked so masculine and beautiful in that moment, his strong cheekbones glowing in the sun. His eyes were the deepest black, eyes she could find herself or lose herself in, and in those eyes she saw the past three years as if through a backwards facing mirror. She saw his pain, his agony, and her own.

But that first eye contact, after so many years, was too much. She ran away before he could say another word, busying herself among the children. For the rest of the feast Amos watched her work, kneeling down to take part in the children's imaginary games. She had suffered so much in his absence. The death of her mother, her father's illness.

But she hadn't married. Amos held onto that. She hadn't married.

Weeks passed. Paul went to see Amos, who gave him a medicine made from ground roots and herbs. Bridget sat firmly in the waiting room, lowering her eyes when Amos exited the small office to tell her his diagnosis.

"I'm sure my father will be able to fill me in just fine," she said, and that was all. This time, she did not make the mistake of eye contact.

Later, in the buggy, she asked her father how he had seemed.

Paul grunted. "Like a perfectly fine doctor. But don't be fooled, Bridget. He will always be a traitor."

They passed weeks like this, Bridget refusing to make eye contact every time she passed Amos in community gatherings or church events. Until, on the day of the first frost, their only cauldron cracked a leak an hour before dinner time.

"I know we should have replaced it earlier," said Bridget, mentally cursing her father for his stinginess.

"Don't worry, dear," said Paul, "I'll go."

But Bridget's father had recently taken turn for the worse, and he looked grey and pinned down in the bed. She gently but firmly pushed him back into the bed, then vanished into her room to pull on her best woolen dress.

"I'll go," she said. Her father began to protest - it wasn't proper for a young lady to travel by herself in growing snowfall. Some would argue, not allowed.

But Bridget gave her father a stern and determined look. Paul said nothing, taken aback. She was growing far too headstrong to make a good Amish wife. This must, he thought, be the result of Amos's brief reappearance. He made a mental note to begin looking for husbands as soon as he possibly could.

"At least take Lydia with you," he shouted after her retreating back, but she was already gone.

By herself, Bridget attached the horse to the buggy and pulled herself up. She tapped the horse lightly on the shoulder with a whip, and it responded immediately, treading gently on the half-frozen ground. As they turned out of the small country road to the larger one, Bridget saw that it was snowing harder than she thought, and the snow collected on the path in clumps that hardened immediately to ice. She kept one hand tight to the reigns, and the other on her whip, which she flicked gently and periodically. As she cantered along, Bridget thought, almost unwillingly, about Amos. How long could she keep avoiding him? Why wouldn't he just leave - he had before, hadn't he?

She closed her eyes, and saw the entire length of his body, modestly clad, the strong shoulders and chin. She unwillingly entered into a memory of her late childhood, when she was just becoming a woman, when they had spoken for hours on the front porch, both neglecting farmwork, both of them smiling foolishly at each other. He had such a beautiful, broken, smile. She had been sure in that moment that she would grow up and marry that man.

She shook her head, eyes still closed. Tried to change his face in her mind to that of any of the other eligible bachelor's in town, even to the face of a model in a glossy magazine she had seen left by the road, where the Robinsons did their tours, but nothing worked.

She was trapped, she was...

CRASH. She was tilting, swaying, falling, crashing. Bridget realized that the horse had wandered off the street in her moment of contemplation. *How could you be so stupid*, she screamed at herself. In slow motion, she tumbled out of the buggy. The horse screamed and bucked at the wheel, which broke in two. Bridget felt a warm gash on her arm before the earth slid slowly away.

She awoke to the sensation of floating, almost dreamily. She was in someone's arms, her legs curled up near her chest, swaying weakly in the cold air. For a moment she felt fear - then a deep, blissful calm overtook her. The arms were strong and gentle. They did not mean her harm.

Dreamily, only slightly aware of a pain on her arm, she looked up at the face of her savior - to find herself caught in the bottomless black stare of the village doctor, the best memory of her childhood, the man who stole her heart. Amos. "Are you ok?" he asked, peering down into her face like he could fall into her.

His face suddenly threw Bridget into hysterics. She had tried so hard to avoid this man and now - to be swaddled in his arms like a *child*. "Let go of me!" she cried out, struggling swiftly and with uncharacteristic anger. "I'm *fine*. I can handle this, I can get Papa or Lydia or-"

As she struggled, her shift rose up her legs. Amos deftly pulled it back down with one hand, preserving her modesty. "Bridget. Bridget listen to me." His voice was warm and assertive.

She quieted. "Can you walk?" he asked her. She nodded, anger still rising red behind her eyes. Amos put her gently down.

"Thank you for your concern," she said coldly. "I should be going now." She looked around. The horse had run off, and the buggy knelt brokenly on the frozen ground, spokes snapped in half.

"Don't be ridiculous," said Amos, "My home isn't far from here. Let me patch you up - I have the materials."

Bridget looked at him, shocked. "You want me to go alone to your home? I don't know what you learned in the outside world but-" Amos looked like he was going to laugh, "-and *what* could possibly be so funny about this?" From her peripheral vision, she saw blood drop to the ground. She wasn't hurt badly, but there was a disproportionate amount of blood.

"I'm sorry," said Amos, "I didn't mean to laugh. But my mother is home, Bridget. I know you're not that kind of girl." A brief pause. "I wouldn't care so much about you if you were."

"That's *rich*, Amos," said Bridget. His name sounded disconcertingly familiar in her mouth, "You care about *me*? You care about your doctor's salaries and your outside girls and your-"

Amos cut her off again. "You have a right to be angry, I don't contest that. You have a right to never speak to me again. But if you'll never talk to me again - at least let me take care of your arm."

Bridget looked down at the dripping wound. It was two miles to her father's farm, which was a long way to travel in the snow with an open wound. And even once she arrived, they lacked the proper materials, the boiled gauze and sharp antiseptic. "Fine," she snapped, "lead the way."

As they walked through the snow, they looked almost comical. He walked so easily through the drifts, his hard boots pounding assuredly on the banks of snowfall. She, on the other hand was stumbling and disoriented, not from the pain on her arm, which was diminishing, but from pure anger. How dare he come back into her life like this? How dare he thwart all her attempts to be rid of him?

They approached Amos's house, which she had only visited once or twice in her childhood. It was rather small - their plot was tiny compared to Bridget and her father's. Amos's mother looked out from the front window, smiling toothlessly (she had lost all her teeth in a battle with jaundice as a teenager), and waving. Bridget waved back, smiling a little herself at the enthusiasm of the greeting.

"Oh, Bridget, it is so lovely to see you," said Amos's mother as soon as she crossed the threshold, "but oh! you've hurt yourself."

"It's nothing," assured Bridget, a little stiffly.

"My Amos will fix you up right away. Oh, it is lovely to see you two friends again."

"I don't know if you would call us friends," replied Bridget, embarrassed.

"Mother, don't smother the girl," called Amos from the other room, "Bridget, if you could come in here, please?"

Bridget nodded politely to Amos's mother and tentatively walked through the threshold. The next room was clearly Amos's office, where her father had been treated weeks before. Amos was holding a thin needle over the candle's flame. Bridget gulped, "what's *that* for?" she asked.

"That's a pretty nasty cut, Bridget," answered Amos, still concentrating, "it'll need stitches." He gestured absent-mindedly to the empty share besides him. "Sit down."

She did as he asked. When he was done sterilizing the needle, he sat down opposite her and held her forearm in one of his. He sewed her up methodically and carefully, not speaking. It hurt less than she thought, but it still hurt. It wasn't until he had begun dressing the wound that Bridget allowed herself to look around. The room was full of shelves and cabinets, full of gauze and water, antiseptic and some pills and bottles she had never seen before.

"Are those from out of town?" she asked, looking at some of those colorful pills, a mix of admiration and accusation in her voice.

Amos looked where she was pointing. "Some of them, yes."

"You know," Bridget said, "Old Doctor Gary didn't use anything from the outside world."

Amos shook his head. "I don't belong to the outside world, but it isn't as bad as people say. There's a lot of sin, yes, but they have the most incredible medicines. Things that can disappear a lifetime of pain in a single moment. The sin and solitude of that world disgusts me. But if their medicine can save even one of the people I love," his eyes flicked up to meet Bridget's, "then they're worth breaking a couple rules for."

"There are people who would expel you for that thought."

"There are more people who like having a doctor who knows what he's doing."

Bridge quieted. She could hear the sounds of Amos's mother rummaging in the kitchen, the sounds of slicing and boiling. It was near dinner time, and the cloudy sky had dimmed in its furious gray hue.

"If the outside world is so great," Bridget's voice broke, cracked in half, almost died. She continued in a whisper. "If the outside world is so great, why didn't you stay away?"

Amos was quiet for a long time. He had finished wrapping up Bridget's arm and ran his arms gently up and down the bandaged area. "Do you remember that summer when we were kids and we found the wild dog who had given birth in the woods?"

"I remember."

"Remember how I wanted to steal the puppies for ourselves. How great would it be to have our own puppies, I told you. And it really was a perfectly ordinary piece of cruelty for a child to partake in. I'm certain I wasn't alone in this."

"But I convinced you to leave them alone."

"You said that it wasn't our place to take these children from their mothers. You said they needed her."

"They did."

"You went home, then. And - you don't know this - I took one anyway. I kept it in my room so you wouldn't know. For three days. Until one day it looked at me, making sad little yelping sounds. I went down to the wood where I knew the dog lived, in that little hollow under the tree, and I put it down there. I waited for hours to make sure nothing attacked it. And, as the sun went under the horizon, the mother dog came back. It took the little one inside the hollow, and that was that."

"What's your point?" Asked Bridget, trying to be combative but failing at the soft sound of his voice.

"You have always been the better person," He clasped her hand in his and looked straight into her eyes," I left because I was selfish and stupid, and for the years I was out there I couldn't look at anything without seeing your face - the sun, dogs, I couldn't even smell grass."

"Then why didn't you come back *sooner*?" she asked, her voice in a hush. She had tightened her grip on his hand.

"I thought you would hate me for it. I thought I had lost you forever. But I know now that love never expires. You might never forgive me but I will never stop loving you. I - oh, lord forgive me - I want to marry you."

"You left me."

"I will never leave again."

"When my mother died I was alone."

"I want to spend the rest of my life making that up to you. Taking care of you. Providing you with comforts and children."

"Amos - how can I? After everything? How can I?" She was crying, hot tears tracking down her cheekbones.

"I know you love me too, undeserving as I am. I can't imagine a life without this love. Can you?"

Bridget was quiet. "I think I need to leave now. The snow's died down and It's only a couple miles to the farm. Papa will be getting worried."

"Ok," said Amos, helping her onto her feet. He gave her a cauldron to borrow (the purpose of her trip anyway) and a bottle of something to dab on the wound. At the door, Bridget suddenly spun around and drew herself close to his face. She could feel the heat of his chest and arms, tense as though poise for embrace.

"Amos," she said, her lips chapped from cold but still pink and shapely, "My father tells me that Eliot will propose marriage soon. What would you do if I said yes? Would you leave again?"

Amos let out a shaky breath. "No, Bridget. I would let you have your love and your family. But as long as you are in this town I will be here also. And if I cannot marry you, I will not marry." Amos shut the door gently, looking almost as surprised as Bridget at the truth of this sudden statement.

Bridget stood in the cold for a second longer, then began the long walk home.

"I'm not comfortable with you going to town by yourself any longer," Paul told Bridget from the sunken spot on the bed where he had been resting all weekend, "it's time you chose a husband."

He had been suspicious around her ever since she came home with no horse, no buggy, and a carefully bandaged arm. His suspicion grew, even though she retrieved and repaired the buggy by asking for help in town, even as she found the runaway horse grazing in a nearby pasture. It reached a boiling point two weeks after her injury, when she returned to Amos to have her stitches removed. "You're so good with fixing the animals' wounds," he said, "can't you take the stitches out yourself?"

She said nothing. And when she came back, Paul was waiting for her with a list of the most eligible bachelors'.

"The Sing is next week," Paul reminded her, "I told Eliot he could look forward to being there."

"Eliot?" asked Bridget, her voice fading slightly. Amos had removed her stitches in silence, and there in the candlelit darkness, each of his subtle touches felt like an eternal promise. Paul didn't know, but where she had previously taken such pains to avoid Amos, she now took pains to encounter him wherever she could. A dialogue of love had sprung up patchwork between them, made entirely of niceties exchanged in the marketplace, a door held open on the way to church, fierce eye contact made as their buggies passed on a busy road. Only once had they truly spoken; walking off together after church, not so far as to be scandalous.

"I don't know how you may still feel about me, but I can sense a softening in your eyes," Amos had whispered.

"I...I feel my anger giving. Leaving, slowly. I feel myself...believing you? Am I crazy?"

Amos smiled. "If you're this crazy already, I want to tell you something."

"What?"

"Next week at the Sing, I'm going to ask you to marry me."

"What? So soon?"

"It's still far too late," he leaned down, his mouth pink and parted slightly, and for a moment Bridget was happy to kiss, to be like the outside women who succumb so easily to love.

"Amos," she said, pushing away, "people will talk." She gathered her skirts up and picked her way towards the church.

"Bridget!" called Amos, "is that a no?" He could see in her eyes that it was not.

As Bridget stared down Paul, who had just suggested - no, commanded - her to dance with Eliot at the Sing, and by extension, to allow him to court her, marry her, fill her with children and take her into the house. She wasn't sure if she was ready to marry Amos. But she didn't know if she could marry at all.

"Papa," she said, "I don't know if I can-"

Paul interrupted her, "That you're what? Ready? You were ready enough to walk off with Amos into the woods last Sunday. You were ready enough to visit him *by yourself* to get your stitches out!"

"Would you have me untreated by the village doctor?" cried out Bridget, her voice almost cracking, "would you rather have me sick, dying, than see this man, who is not as bad as you might think?"

Paul waited until her crying subsided - she did not realize that she was crying, the tears had slipped out in a moment of panic. "Bridget," he said calmly, "Amos is not a good match for you. He is tainted by the outside world. Eliot is a good man, strong, he will provide for you."

"Why do I have to get married at all?" cried out Bridget.

"I have already done you a great injustice by keeping you at home. But Lydia is a capable child, on the cusp of womanhood. When you marry, she will be able to take over the farm, and her brothers can take over once she marries."

Bridget was silent.

"Bridget," repeated Paul, "do not lose faith. This boy has been sent down to tempt you. Eliot will give you peace."

The next few weeks passed quickly, with Bridget once again avoid Amos. He seemed distraught at the change, several times reaching towards her in an unseemly way that made people shake their heads as they past. She would dodge his outstretched hand. She hoped that by avoiding him so strenuously, he would get the message; he could no longer propose at the Sing.

The morning of the sing, she dressed in her best, most modest clothes. She braided her hair carefully, and even let Lydia string those braids with beads. It was a clear, cool morning. She went downstairs to see her father dressed as handsomely as ever, a little unsteady on his feet but proud and tall.

"This is an important day, Bridget," Paul said to her as they (they whole family) piled into the buggy and their long-suffering horse, unused to carrying so many at once, pulled out of the little road. Bridget said nothing, and watched the countryside sway past.

At the swing, the table was laden with the fruits of the harvest and fiddlers were tuning their instruments. Bridget sat gently on a seat while everyone else bustled about, chattering with their friends they hadn't seen in church. "Bridget!" shouted Lydia, "come make a daisy chain with me!"

Bridget smiled weakly. "Maybe later, dear."

Paul stood firmly by Bridget, looking stern. When Amos came to say hello, Pau shot him a look of such venom that he quickly backed off.

But Bridget could see a steely will in his eyes. Then Eliot came to pay his respects. He was a nice boy, with a broad, almost goofy face.

"Good morrow, Bridget," he said, speaking in the old-fashioned tongue of their ancestors, "how are you on this beautiful day?"

"Well," answered Bridget, curtly. Eliot looked up nervously at Paul, and chuckled a bit. Paul gave him a reassuring pat on the shoulder.

"We'll talk later," he said, "there'll be plenty of time for you to get to know each other in the coming months." When Paul had left, he leaned down to catch Bridget's ear. "What's wrong with you, daugther?" he hissed, "this is a good man. Why do you scorn him?"

"Papa," started Bridget, her eyes brimming with tears, "I've realized something about who I want to marry. I've realized..."

"Time for the dance!" someone yelled from the other side of the field, and immediately there was a ruckus drowning out Bridget's small voice. The chair was practically yanked out from underneath her, and immediately there was a great rush of limbs and smiles. She numbly remembered her dancing steps, and was quickly swung from partner to partner; her father, the old horse doctor, then Eliot's dumbly smiling face.

"Isn't this lovely?" he yelled at her, "the two of us dancing together?"

But before she had a chance to reply, partners changed again, and she found herself spinning gently in a circle with Amos. He didn't say anything, but he gave her a long, low, look, a look of absolute love and pain, and in turn Bridget found her own pain surfacing beyond the music and the dance, and she wanted nothing more than to be alone with him for a while, to just sit with him and love him.

Suddenly, a voice rose above the crowd. "Excuse me!" shouted the lead fiddler, "I believe we have a special announcement to be made!"

Bridget looked at Amos, horrorstruck (and perhaps a little hopeful). "What did you-"

"It wasn't me," whispered Amos urgently, "Bridget, whatever happens-"

Bridget was suddenly yanked away by the strong arm of her father. As he pulled her through the crowds of people, she noticed his breath sounded ragged, tired, his lungs rising and falling with something close to a rattle. "Papa are you ok?" Paul did not answer, and instead thrust her into the middle of a small clearing the people had formed. Also at the middle, Eliot, who was on one knee.

"Bridget," he said (had his voice always been so nasal, so whiny?), "you may not know me well, but I have watched you from afar. I have seen your strength as you cared for your mother and your sisters, I have seen your gentle grace through suffering."

As he continued his monologue, Bridget looked around her. The men and women were smiling, nodding, so full of charity. "And I knew from that moment you would make a wonderful mother for my children," Bridget looked down at Eliot's upturned face. "No," she whispered, "no." Eliot didn't hear here, both those closest to her began muttering. She tried to catch Amos's eyes in the crowd, but she couldn't find him. "No!" she was screaming now, "I can't! I can't!"

There was a collected gasp. Eliot reeled back as though slapped. Bridget's father appeared suddenly near her, and held her face in his hands. "Bridget!" he shouted, "why do you shame me this way? Why do you-" he inhaled gaspingly, with terror. His knees buckled, his face turned blue.

"Papa, are you ok?" cried Bridget, as the knot of people grew ever tighter. Paul collapsed to the floor in a quivering heap. "Papa! Papa!" And then everything for her, too, went black.

Bridget woke up in her own home, awkwardly crunched into an armchair. Her father was asleep in the bed, strange machines hooked up to him. She jolted, then ran up to his body to make sure he was breathing. And he was; slowly, laboriously but breathing. She immediately tried to pull the tubes out of his arm.

"Bridget, no," said a voice. Amos walked through the open door, "leave him be."

"What are these things?" cried out Bridget, "what have you done to him?"

"These are modern appliances," said Amos. "I didn't want to use them, but today they saved your fathers life."

"What happened to him?" asked Bridget, less panicked now that she knew her father was safe.

"He had a heart attack, a minor one. Nothing that rest shouldn't fix. He'll have to eat healthier from now on, and exercise. But I think he has a good many years left in him."

Bridget looked down at her hands. "This is my fault," she said, "I love you, I know I do. It's the simplest thing in the world to me, but look what it's done to my father."

Amos looked away. "Bridget, I never meant to come between you and your duty. If I could take all of this back I would."

"You'd do no such thing," croaked a voice from the bed. Amos and Bridget both gasped in delight. Paul had opened his eyes. "If I could have a moment with my daughter, please."

"Of course," stuttered Amos, "anything you want."

When they were alone, Bridget knelt deeply by her fathers bed and took his hands in hers. "Papa, I am so sorry."

He reached across the bed and put his hand, tough from years of farm labor, on her head. "Child, it was wrong of me to put so much pressure on you. I see now that this Amos cares for you more than Eliot ever will."

"Why do you think that?" asked Bridget, frowning.

"Where is Eliot now? Amos is here, he made the decisions that had to be made, controversial as they are."

Bridget looked down, but Paul cupped her chin in his hand. "I'm tired, Bridget," he said, "I'm tired of keeping my daughter from having what she wants." Bridget stood up shakily, and her father smiled at her.

Slowly, she kissed him on the forehead, and turned to where Amos was waiting for her.

"What did he say?" Amos asked anxiously.

"He said we could be together," Bridget's voice sounded far away to her. "He said he wants us to be happy."

"Bridget!" cried Amos, "That's great news!"

"But Amos!" she looked up at him, tears falling from her eyes, "I don't know if I'm ready yet."

Amos held her hands in his, and looked deep into her beautiful face, the face he had loved so much since childhood. "Bridget," he said, "you don't have to be. I'll wait until you are."

She smiled, shakily, and kissed him. It was only a peck, it was only on the cheek. But in that moment, they both knew that even that small kiss would provide enough comfort for the rest of their days.